MASTERY OF ATTRACTION

ACACIA WARMERDAM

ISBN/SKU: 979-8-3302-9742-9
Imprint: WarRose & Spells
First Printing, 2025

Cover design by: Acacia Warmerdam
Printed in the United States of America
First Printing, 2025

Contents

Triggers & Tropes

Triggers

Infertility- Lite   Pregnancy- Lite   Torture

Tropes

Second Chance/Unrequited Love
Fall in love with the wrong person
Secret royal/partners in crime
Good people have good sex
Sworn off a relationship

I can't help myself...

Scan me ;)

1

A Widow With No Qualms

I don't have many regrets in life. If anything, I enjoy the privacy and independence I have been afforded, so to say I regret this moment would also be an absolute lie. You see, at this very moment, I find myself in a sticky situation—one I do not want to get out of. Because I am letting him do what he pleases with me, in truth I am enjoying it more than I ought to. With every thrust and pulse his body gives me, I give back the same. Wanting him to take over me until I am nothing but a mess of nerves and pleas. In all honesty, I hope I can't get out of bed tomorrow. The further down my throat he shoves his fingers, the more I ache to not think until my climax breaks, and damn, is it my fault for making this man this way...

Two Weeks Ago

It was an ordinary Tuesday; I had finished all my assignments for the day, making sure to write back to each of the unsatisfied ladies or lonely soldiers who sent me fifty or so letters a month. A majority of questions revolved around love & marriage, but sadly, most ask how to enjoy lovemaking or for relationship advice. Some are just in need of a pen pal, especially the soldiers, but almost all send me some type of compensation for a response. Seeing as how I am now widowed with no plans for marriage, this pursuit directly provides me with a voice and, most notably, independence. One would typically say it is scandalous to stay single at this time in high society. If I am not married, I am nothing to the polite association, and yet I am content to be a lowly baroness out of the sight of most gentle persons. Well, besides the crown prince, for he likes any woman with tight corset strings, and he would not fall under the category of *gentle*. However, being a widow, I can write the most scandalous things to these individuals without fear of my precious virtue being questioned. Because they all know I lost that virtue on my wedding night many years ago. Truthfully, my virtue went out the door the second I came of age, and my father could sell me off to the baron—my late husband. Don't get me wrong, Ronald was a good man, soft and kind but very dull. He had little to no personality and often didn't get my jokes. Regardless, he wasn't a vile old age, so I didn't mind sharing a bed with him. If anything, he was very giving, so when he did die, I was devastated. So miserable, in fact, that I didn't attend events for a year and closed myself off from the social world. Even if what we had wasn't love, it was an absolute comfort, and that was what I missed. I missed sharing a bed and a meal, a laugh at the end of a day, and honestly, I missed sex.

As I said, this was an ordinary day with expected letters until I got to the one I had saved for last. Its gold leaf and frills screamed nobility, and aristocrats rarely write to me so openly. They usually hide within plain stationery, not this ostentatious thing. I know they write, but under a fake name, thinking I wouldn't know who they are. But I am not so dense. However, it is fun to pretend not to know these things because as long as I don't show my claws, neither do they.

All was harmonious until I opened that letter, and I had no idea how much it would change my life. "Madam, you have a caller at the door," Janet, my maid, called as she walked into my room, coming to set a small cup of lemon tea down for me to sip on.

"Who is it?" I asked as I slipped my letter opener through the golden paper. I was shocked to see two 1,000-pound notes slid out with a letter penned on woven parchment. "Geez, what is this?" I murmured to myself, unfolding the extravagant paper.

"Some man who said he was sent to speak about a job," Janet explained, looking over the money in surprise before walking back out of the room.

"Send him to the sunroom and set up lunch. I will be down in a moment," I instructed as I turned the letter over, feeling slightly irritated that an unknown call interrupted my day. But all of those thoughts ceased the second I read the first line of the letter.

Dear Madam La'Blauvelt,

Whispers of your exceptional talents have reached my ears, and I find myself in a most delicate predicament, seeking your esteemed assistance. I have commenced the arrangements for my daughter's union with the Archduke of House Sigmund, as per her royal wish.

As you may well know, the archduke is a most enigmatic figure, displaying scant emotion, and there are murmurs regarding his affinities toward the fairer sex. To allay any concerns regarding potential 'heir' matters, I implore you to handle this task with the utmost care and confidentiality. I shall speak plainly: I require you to ascertain that the archduke's inclinations lie with women, ensuring he can bestow his name upon a successor of my lineage. I seek tangible proof of his capabilities, and discretion is paramount, as he shall soon be my son-in-law.

You must observe his prowess firsthand—either through your own eyes or by a trusted proxy. The funds enclosed are intended for the enchantress you select to captivate his interest. Should you choose to undertake this endeavor personally, consider it a gesture of goodwill between our families.

You have a month before the engagement is publicly declared. I trust you shall not disappoint me.

Leave no trace.

F

King Franz

No evidence?

He really expects me to get rid of this letter? This would be my only proof if something were to go awry and the king chose to take my head. I rubbed my neck, leaning back with a groan, anxious about what this endeavor might truly cost if not *just* my life. Now the king even thinks I am a whore who he can send to seduce men. I guess that is the price I will have to pay for liberation, yet I wonder if this was the crown prince's doing. There is no way the king would ever think of me without someone whispering to him these tales of me—for the prince loves to exaggerate. "Janet, are you there?" I called as I got up, folding the letter to put it back in the envelope with the money.

"Yes, Madam, and the man is in the sunroom waiting," she said as she opened the door, looking me over in concern. Her brown eyes and tan skin were soft and youthful for such a strong woman of not even forty that you would never know how devious she could truly be when needed or provoked.

"Take this to the safety deposit box at Ronald's banks, not mine," I ordered, and she took it, no questions asked. It was better to have that in my husband's bank safe, and I doubt if the king became upset with me, he would look there, of all places.

I closed my robe and looked in the mirror, feeling wildly inadequate for this job of seduction. I wonder what Archduke Sigmund likes because that will be the deciding factor here. I have black curly hair, much longer than any other noble lady, since I refuse to follow the trends of the new short hairstyles. By all accounts, I have been told I look adorable with my big green eyes and full lips. My body is toned, and younger men still try to call upon me often, even at the age of twenty and eight. Even then, I do not think I am the archduke's type, especially when so many young women are about to debut this summer. Then again, I have not seen him in over a year, and he has never shown any interest in any woman I know, but therein lies the problem...what does this man like?

I pulled open the bedroom door, strolling lazily to the sunroom, trying to figure out how the king could be all right with me or another seducing his soon-to-be son-in-law. He wrote I have to seduce...not bed. I wonder if that would make me lose my head if I went all the way with the archduke. It doesn't bother me one way or another if he fancies women; I just need to think of a good way to test such a thing.

"Miss, do you need to dress?" the older man shouted as he stood from the chaise, almost falling over from my state of undress.

"Oh, calm down. It is a robe, not a negligee. Why have you come here unannounced on a Tuesday?" I scoffed as I sat across from him, and he openly gaped at the small part of my exposed ankle. This poor old man must just be dying right now.

"I have a file for you on Archduke Sigmund," the man managed to choke out, but his eyes did not leave my ankle as he handed me the thin file—poor, poor man.

"The king works fast. I will give him that," I murmured as I opened the cream-colored envelope to skim over the contents.

- Blond hair, 6'5, blue eyes, weight 220.
- Commander of the three archaic armies
- Combat time 13 years
- 0-7 No losses in battle.
- Only son
- Parents are alive/estranged.
- Anna Sigmund, Chester Sigmund
- Only sister: Gretel Sigmund
- Recluse, short-tempered, never seen with a woman.

"You are bad at your job. Please give me your pen," I requested, and the man fumbled to get it from his pocket as I reached out to take it, waiting with an outstretched hand. "You did not even put his full name in the file. Claud Nulimar Sigmund is not 6'5. He is 6 foot, but he just looks 6'5. Probably when in his battle armor. Regardless of that, I already knew all these things and more. I do not live under a rock," I chastised the older gray man, and he ruffled at my critique.

"Madam, you have—" he began, but I cut him off.

"I am not trying to be rude. I just expected a man of your age, employed by the king, to have more information on this mark. Like perhaps his age, which is thirty and one, by the way," I hummed, "If I am to get close to the Archduke of Sigmund, the oldest family traceable back to three continents,

I need to know very specific things," I declared as I leaned forward to grab a small tea sandwich to eat. He watched me with bitterness, and I get it. He is upset I am telling him how to accomplish his assignment. But he did an abysmal job, and I can't lose in the eyes of the king because of this man's foolishness.

"Then what is it you need to know?" he questioned gruffly.

"Here is your pen. Take notes on this," I ordered as I handed him back the file with the pen, and his face became tight in irritation.

"Find out where he likes to eat when he does go out, ask around his staff what books he likes to read, where does he go when he is not home? What bank does he use, what hair salon, and where does he spend his time when not conquering the battlefield? He is in the capital now. What does he like to do all day?" I teased because this was all simple stuff. "I want to know what he likes. So, for the next few days, I can learn them, or this will be dead before it starts. Life isn't love at first sight. It is arranged marriages and trying to find an escape. I need to know what his escape is," I explained, and to his credit, the old man was taking notes.

"You live up to your reputation," the man grumbled as he stood, grabbing a sandwich to take with him.

"Let's hope for both our heads that you do a better job. I don't believe the king is especially forgiving," I warned as he toddled out of the room. "Of all the men the king wants me to seduce, why does it have to be Claude?" I muttered as my hand rubbed over my neck again.

2

Angering the Archduke

I have only formally met Claude once when I was seventeen, and he was twenty. We have been in each other's company at events since then but never had more than an introduction or casual glance. Maybe once, I was in the same circle as the archduke during a conversation, but only when Ronald was around years ago or the prince was being cheeky. Regardless, the only time I even conversed with him personally was after he had gone off to war for a few years and returned unharmed, so naturally, the king threw a party to celebrate *'the glory of the capitals'* return. Even then, Claude was the most attractive man I had ever seen, and at that age, I was *looking a lot,* hoping to find myself an exemplary match. On that night, I still remember how he stood stoically beside the king, refusing to come anywhere near the dance floor, and avoided conversing with any of the ladies or the princess who had incessantly nagged him for any attention. People said he was callous, but when I watched him, I felt pity for him. He must have seen something tragic enough never to let a smile creep on his face even once. War can do that to you; it's what killed my brother before he died, first the despair of it, and then the battle finally won out. War kills not only the body but also the mind—with that depressing thought of my brother dying in the war, I started to drink. While we celebrated one man coming home, thousands lay dead in Calaiva, the country refusing to give back the bodies, never letting me bury my brother beside our mother. That night was the only time I spoke to the archduke directly, and it would not win me any favor. But in my drunken haze, the exchange went something like this.

Somehow, I had made my way to the second-story veranda, trying to escape my father, now relentlessly trying to marry me off because he lost his heir. I probably would have had more of a choice if my brother Paul hadn't died, but as I said, Ronald wasn't a horrible choice on my father's end. At the time, I was nearly eighteen, which only gave me less than a year to find a match he approved of...naively, I believed I had a choice.

When I walked out on the veranda, I never even noticed Claude was there. If I weren't drinking, I probably would have seen him and left him be. Though, the most embarrassing part of this whole thing was that I was crying. I hadn't cried in front of anyone besides my family, and he saw me—*sobbing* over the idea of dead bodies rotting in a marsh, unable to come home.

At first, the archduke was charming. "Miss, are you hurt?" he had asked, and I turned in shock to see him standing in the shadows on the other side of the veranda. I was delirious from drinking, and I wiped off my face quickly in embarrassment, only to see that he looked miserable as well.

"No, but you are," I agonized with an uncomfortable laugh. I still remember how his blue eyes flashed as he pulled his sword, placing it at my chest, right between my breasts. The cold of the metal was jarring even while drunk.

"Was that a threat," he gritted his teeth so hard I could see the rage in his jaw, and I laughed. I LAUGHED AT HIM! Like the threat wasn't real—like he was joking.

"I meant in your eyes. You are hurting, like Paul. He was always unhappy," I lamented as I pushed the blade away from my chest, not scared at all of this man because he lives by a knight's code, and they would never harm a lady unless threatened. That was my rationalization in this chaotic moment.

"Paul?" he questioned as he sheathed his sword, moving to look over me more carefully. His hand reached out to pull my chin toward the light from the open door. His thumb pushed my tear across my cheek, and I remember the madness in his stare, one that made me realize I was unchaperoned with a man for the first time in my life. "You have the same eyes," he noted as he looked at me in what seemed like disgust before striding from the veranda, leaving me alone.

After that, I only saw him here and there at parties that the king coerced him to attend, and never once did he seem to recognize me or apologize for that night we first met. So now I am to seduce the archduke, and I have no idea how to break this man's walls so that the crazy princess can get a chance to woe him. I was surprised that Princess Flora still desired him with how adamant he had been never to take a wife. Now that his sister has had a son, there is an heir to fulfill the Sigmund rule with their aging father's inevitable demise looming over their house. So it appears he has no marriage aspirations and needs none. But that princess...if she gets her way, there will never be a more ill-suited match in all of history. She truly is a vile human.

* * *

I was surprised when the investigator returned only four days later with a file a half-inch thick. He handed it to me with a smug grin that I didn't pester him for because he did a good job even if I had to hold his hand. "He eats every Wednesday at Masoin Dejor at six and is always in bed by 9. Monday through Friday, he is at the state building for work now that he is retired from active duty. He is in by seven in the morning and out by five thirty, sometimes six at night if the crown prince comes by, which is becoming more frequent. Saturday, he sometimes goes to a bookshop on 3rd Street if he has finished the previous book on time. Sunday, he does not leave his home," the old man declared, and I set down the file to look over his red cheeks and brown eyes in delight.

"Continue," I voiced kindly as I became slightly proud of him.

"The archduke prefers hard liquor and doesn't care for sweets—" he stated, and that I could get behind, I'd eat something salty over sweet any time. "—and he *is* 6'5," the man assured me, and I began to chuckle.

"I guess I will get to measure him in the end," I jested, making the man blush red, darker than the roses on my wallpaper.

"Anyways, there are more tedious things in the file, but he takes his nephew to the track every two weeks to watch the dog races. He doesn't bet," at that, I leaned forward with a grin.

"How amazing," I murmured, and of all things, I was surprised that I had never seen him there before because I had never missed a race besides this last year after my husband's passing. "You did well," I praised him. The race would be in two days, and it felt like fate had possibly given me a hand with this one, but I could have used any of the other places to engage with him. But this one felt less of a lie and more organic of an encounter.

Two Days Later

Out of dignity, I did not go overboard with my primping because I quite possibly am not his type. So today, I will have to try my hardest to get him alone at some point so that I can throw myself at him while still making it feel natural. I do like kids, so I could possibly try to get on his good side by way of his nephew Lloyd. "Madam, the archduke's carriage is just there," Janet exclaimed as she stood to look out of the window for me when we had pulled up to the parking field. "And a spot is open close to it," Janet grinned before telling my coachman Thomas where to park.

I got out, seeing the Sigmund crest on the side of the black carriage a row away, and grinned at Janet, us both relishing the plan coming together so excellently. However, the carriage would be the last part of the plan. "Perhaps make sure the wheels are very well looked after," I hummed to Janet before I turned to look for Claude by the dog track. I usually head to the right of the stands towards the cheaper of the seats, but this time, I made my way toward the high-end boxes. I imagine I had never seen them here before because I never came this way and never desired to. It did have a better view, but I never bet, and I could see fine from my brother's box.

It wasn't long before I saw them standing in line to place a bet, and I had to admit that Claude was handsome to the point I was already distracted. He was so tall...that I already knew, but his dirty, blond hair was pushed back flawlessly to highlight his strong face with just enough sharp lines that he didn't look like a caveman I had seen in a book. He walked a fine line between burly and noble, which was hard to find; most men now were too soft for my tastes, but he was better than carved marble, handsome enough he should be painted.

I flattened out my dark green dress before walking to the ice cream stand to get two vanilla cones. Now, here is where the artifice commences. "Janet?" I called softly as I moved toward the archduke, knowing she was nowhere close, and thanks to the heat, the sweet treat would begin to soften and soon make a mess. "Janet?" I called again and groaned as I pretended to look around the crowd while moving closer toward the child who looked so much like his uncle you wouldn't know they weren't father and son. That dirty blond hair was so striking it was easy to see who they were from afar, and his size was imposing. "Ugh, Janet," I complained as the ice cream ran down my fingers, and I stopped just before bumping into the small boy, feigning shock to have almost run into them. "I'm so sorry," I apologized as I looked at the slumping ice cream in irritation, "Oh, young master, would you take this as an apology before it is ruined? I almost knocked you down while looking for my maid," I explained as I knelt down in front of the archduke's nephew Lloyd, who must only be five. He looked up at me excitedly with the same blue eyes as his uncle, but the boys were excited...got him.

"Please, uncle," the boy begged. I slowly glanced up to see the archduke's piercing blue stare, which would scare off most. It even stilled my breath, which I hoped he assumed was shock.

"Oh, archduke, I didn't see it was you," I lied as casually as I could muster before his eyes narrowed to look at the ice cream melting down my fingers.

"It's dripping," he remarked, his voice so deep it temporarily took me aback, but the boy began to whine, drawing my attention.

"Oh gosh, it is," I exclaimed before licking the one in my right hand in a circle, and I watched the archduke's eyes to see if he had any reaction. I was shocked that his eyebrow cocked up, and he nodded yes curtly, so I wasn't going to waste that opportunity. "Here you go," I offered sweetly as I bent down to give the boy the treat that was presumed to be for Janet.

"Thank you. Miss," the boy hummed politely as the line moved up, and I took a step with them, drawing Claude's eyes. He doesn't like me here...I can feel it.

"She has been married and is too old to be a miss. She is a madam," the archduke said dryly, and the dig was so unwarranted I almost lost my composure.

"Yes, it is probably best you call me widow. Or is that insensitive?" I quipped, and he scrutinized me with those cold eyes, hoping he did not see that his words wounded me.

The boy pointed out at the track, drawing my attention as you could see the dogs all waiting behind the stations. "Did you pick a dog? I like Bruce," the boy turned to ask me, giving me the opportunity to step up with them once again, thankfully breaking the tension.

"I have not. I just like to watch. My brother and I used to come as kids, so I never bet, but I hope Bruce does well for you, young master," I spoke kindly as I took another lick of my melting ice cream, and if my hand gets more sticky, I'll have to leave to wash up, ruining this moment.

"Me too. Uncle said Bruce has good breeding, so he should be fast," the boy exclaimed, and I chuckled at his words, trying to stifle a grin.

"What was funny about that?" Claude asked, and I looked up at him, no longer hiding my amusement.

"Those words can be taken out of context in many ways, my lord," I teased as the boy approached the ticket counter.

"100 on Bruce," the boy sang, bouncing around while licking his ice cream.

"Your chaperon must agree," the clerk voiced nervously, looking at the archduke, knowing precisely who he was.

"Double it for me. I think you are right, little master," I announced as I reached to grab money from my wallet, but the archduke set it down first. "I can pay my share," I offered, but he took the stub before I could protest and led us to the side of the track.

"It is fine," Claude stated before he handed me my ticket, and I took it with a frown, knowing that this was my queue to leave.

I truthfully don't like to bet, so I bent low and gave my stub to the boy, hoping it would also earn me more favor with his uncle. "I think you will have better luck holding on to it. You see, I have horrible luck," I laughed as I stood up, bowing to him, "It was lovely to meet you, little duke," I announced, and I was actually sorry to have to go. The kid was lovely, while the archduke was like a wall of ice.

"Stay. We have a box," the boy offered excitedly as he finished his ice cream, and I felt Claude's eyes burning into me like he was willing me to be gone.

"No, this looks like a very special day for you both. I have a box, but way on the other side," I explained as I pointed across the track. "So I better be going before I am deemed an interloper," I joked before bowing to them both.

"Goodbye," Claude said curtly.

"Goodbye, widow," the boy called cheerfully, and I couldn't stop my body from flinching, for I did not predict that attack from a child. Never in my life did I expect a child to say something like that to me so boldly and with a smile.

"He didn't mean it with malice. He is very young. They are still teaching him how to address people," Claude offered an excuse, which was shocking and unexpected. Despite my upset, I smiled at the boy, too embarrassed to meet Claude's cold eyes.

"I know, malice is for the grown-ups," I muttered as I walked away, and thankfully, I could see Janet smiling at me from 10 feet around the track.

"He is watching you walk away," she whispered to me before she linked my arm and wove me through the throngs of people. I threw the melted treat in a bin we passed beside the track much too aggressively, unable to hide my offense.

"How long did he watch me?" I asked, and she grinned wider.

"At least ten seconds until the boy distracted him," she noted. "I think he even smiled,"

"Good. So now you will need to get a ride back with someone. I just hope this works," I groaned, still feeling the tension from his eyes and the sting of the boy's words.

Bruce did not win, but everything else was going to plan since Janet had broken the wheel on the carriage without anyone seeing and made her way home with the pretense of bringing another carriage to get me. So I waited with my coachman Thomas, looking at the damage, proud that Janet made it look like an accident. Suddenly, I heard the sound of little running feet, and I knew that my plan was about to pass or fail here at the races. "Madam, he did not win. I am not lucky either," the boy shouted as he dashed up beside me, looking at my broken wheel with me.

"Well, today might just be the day for it," I sighed as I pulled off my sun hat to fan myself, not only because it was hot but so Claude would see my breasts better from where he now loomed beside me. Maybe he is 6'5...

"We can give you a ride," Claude offered, and that was shocking. I figured the boy would have to ask after I harped on about it.

"I am not really in a position to object. Thank you so much for your kindness," I said before turning to my coachman. "Thomas, will you tell Janet I got a ride home, and please ensure she eats with you? It will be late when you both get home," I ordered before walking toward the archduke, who was monitoring me carefully. His blue eyes were piercing and so wildly confusing. I felt judged, as if he knew this was a trick.

"Will do, madam. Be safe," Thomas called as I walked to the other carriage, and Claude's gaze never left me. Is this prickly feeling I have guilt or fear?

The archduke was quiet as he opened the door for me, but when I went to get in, I didn't see him holding out his hand to help me until it was too late to receive it. Darn, that would have been the perfect time to touch him; I internally groaned as I took off my hat to fan myself again. "Madam, did you see Durango? He was so fast. Next time, I will bet on him," the boy said excitedly, and I smiled at him as Claude got into the carriage, making it tilt from his considerable size.

"He was very fast. However, I was partial to Bon. He was very steady. That is a good quality," I declared, and the boy nodded before turning in the seat to look out the window at the race track as the carriage moved forward. His little feet kicked joyously, and sometimes it hurt to see such precious children when all I ever wanted was one; I considered with a melancholy smile that I didn't mean to reveal.

"I will take you home second. Your estate is farther away than his," Claude informed me, and I nodded.

"How do you know where I live?" I asked, and he glared at me openly, and anxiety prickled my chest.

"I knew your husband," he declared, but he really had no idea where I lived now because I wasn't at the La'Blauvelt estate any longer.

"I see," I whispered as I looked to Llyod, who had turned so he was facing me now, and that was the end of any conversation between him and me, which was fine because I didn't want to explain how my dead husband's cousin Chal had thrown me out of the estate after Ronald's passing.

"We usually play a game on the way home," the boy said, and I smiled at the child, who was easy to spend time with, unlike his uncle. Even if the archduke was upset with me, by the end of this, at least it was a good day. Despite the archduke's cold attitude toward me, the ride back with the little duke was proving delightful. "What goes up but never comes back down?" he asked, his excitement infectious.

I pondered for a moment but was not quick enough when the archduke said, "Age," and Llyod huffed in upset.

"Give her a chance," Llyod groused as he turned more toward me, and it was hard not to smile at the boy.

"I think I can keep up," I hummed, taking a moment to think of something that would test the archduke in a different way. "I'm always on the dinner table, but you don't get to eat me. What am I?" I said, hoping the double meaning was veiled well.

"A fork?" Llyod asked, and I shrugged.

"I will take it, but I was looking for silverware," I noted. We continued like this for ten minutes while the archduke scowled.

For such a young boy, Llyod was surprisingly witty and very good at riddles. He almost got me with, 'What has many ears but can't hear,' I dare say I would have been mortified if I had not thought of corn as he was getting out of the carriage.

When Claude got out of the cab to return the child, he offered no reference of time for his return, and it took him at least fifteen minutes to get back. When the coach took off again, the atmosphere was tense and honestly unnerving now that his nephew wasn't here. "What do you want from me?" Claude asked after five minutes of silence, and I was glad for any talking. I was beginning to stress that my plan would fail with how little we conversed. That and he was going to take me to the wrong place, somewhere I never wanted to go to again.

"If I tell the truth, you won't believe me," I teased, and for a second, I swore I saw his lip curve up.

"Then tell me something I will believe," he demanded, yet his tone wasn't nearly as biting, so I needed to watch myself to hopefully keep him in a better mood.

"My only goal now is to tempt you, my lord," I hummed, which wasn't a lie.

"To kill me?" he asked curtly, and I was shocked by his quick tone change.

"Why do you keep accusing me of strange things?" I questioned, my feelings hurt again like the one other time we met—that ended with a blade at my breast.

"Then why have you pursued me?" he challenged, and I was offended because I am meticulous. He should have no reason to believe I sought him out. Even if I do have a growing file on him back home, he doesn't know that. I looked out the door and knew this was only going to get worse because he didn't trust me at all.

"I am only a few blocks away. Drop me here, for I do not feel safe with you," I ordered. He leaned in to look at me closely, curling his lip terrifyingly.

"At least that wasn't a lie," he hummed as if he could read my mind before he leaned back.

"I haven't lied to you once," I snapped, and that was true, but only my words were true since I had deceived him to get to this point.

"Yet you approached me and are now in my charge after us only having talked once before. So this is just coincidence?" the archduke challenged like he didn't believe me, and it was infuriating how shrewd he was.

"Believe what you will," I murmured before crossing my legs to distract him, making the hem pull up on my dress, but when I glanced, he was looking at my face, not my legs. Shit, this will be impossible. I need more time to wear him down. I pulled the hem up more as I gripped my dress and went back to fanning my chest. If it didn't distract him, it at least calmed me down.

"I will give you ten minutes to explain to me once we get to your house, or you will never see me again. However, if I feel threatened, I will kill you," he warned, and I sighed loudly, rolling my eyes and slamming my hat down on the bench seat.

"Fine," I muttered as I rubbed my neck, upset at him for assuming I wanted to kill him. "But take me to your house. I do not wish to be killed in front of my staff, and I assume it will be easier for you to cover it up at your house," I retorted, hoping he saw the joke in my words, but he only stared at me before tapping three times on the roof.

"You are very strange," he stated just as the carriage turned left away from downtown and toward his estate.

3

An Unexpected Discovery

If he can already see through this scheme of mine, I have no choice but to lie or tell him the truth. Both seem like treacherous options, especially with the possibility of him killing me. The whole way to his office, where I assumed he was leading me, I debated between the two options, and since it took a ridiculously long time to get there, I was happy to have a moment to think because I was at a loss for how to approach him. Yet, I kept becoming distracted by the expanse of his estate. Compared to my old mansion with Ronald, which was considerable in size, my whole first floor could fit in this corridor. It seemed remarkably unreasonable to have so much vacant space, and I have a feeling his office would be the size of my whole townhouse. Thankfully, it would be easy to find my way out since there were no turns, just one long hall with hundreds of windows. "This must get old," I murmured under my breath when we finally got to a door at least five minutes later, and I had not seen one person yet, not even a maid. My palms began to sweat as I moved to sit on a couch across from him in the enormous, ornately decorated study that was ill-suited for his presence. Every wall was covered in what I assumed were family photos, all trimmed in gold.

He didn't offer to help me sit or even indicate that there would be tea service, and I do not feel that he is going to be hospitable in the least during whatever this is going to be. "Sit," he commanded as I was smoothing the back of my dress to do just that. Mercifully, he had spoken first, giving me something to work with, even if it was more hostility. Hostility was better than silence.

"I was your grace," I teased him as I folded my hands in my lap to look unaffected when a knock sounded at the door, startling me while he seemed to expect it. He got up and received a small tray with only one cup. His staff must not know he has a visitor. I wonder if he brought me in a secret way because we didn't enter through what I imagine would be the main doors, and we came in through a small door off the stables.

He returned to set the tea down between us on a small table, and he pushed the full cup toward me before going to a small serving table beside a desk to grab another. When he sat back in front of me, he looked down at his empty cup expectantly, like he wanted me to pour him the tea, so instead,

I chose to lean back and sip mine with a smug grin. I wasn't ready to cater to this man, and his indifference was stifling. In such an extensive room, I felt suffocated by his gaze.

"Are you trying to kill my nephew?" he questioned after another minute of silence, and I slowly set down the cup of tea to look back into his cold eyes.

"No," I snapped, not hiding my offense, and he leaned back, crossing his legs, loosening his tie, distracting me. It didn't help that he was so alluring in his dark-brown tweed suit. He slowly took off his gloves, and I feared I would die from heat exhaustion as I watched how he bit the tips of the glove to pull them down his long fingers. I gulped hard and had to hide my body's reaction to how seductive he was being. When he undid his top button and leaned back on the couch opposite me, my face began to feel hot as I objectified him.

"I will give you one chance to prove to me you are not a threat," he offered, and I was pleased to get words out of him again, yet I needed my wits if I was about to start my plan. I need not be the wound-up one...I must be the seductress and pretend that I am not terrified and turned on right now.

"For the next ten minutes, I ask you to trust me," I voiced softly as I slowly stood and began to unbutton my dress at the front, drawing his attention. I hid my anxiety well, not wanting him to see how timid I was to bear my body to him; I could not let him see my fingers tremble. This was my one shot, so I could not afford to lose his curiosity. "I will give you assurance I hold no weapons, but I ask only one thing," I whispered as I let the dress slide down my body so I was in only my undergarments. A set of black lacies I was grateful that I put on since I never expected to get this far today. I stepped towards him, his eyes observing me like I was a wild animal ready to attack him. "You must be restrained for my security. Men tend to get handsy," I offered with a chuckle as an excuse, and his gaze narrowed on my body. The black lingerie should tempt any straight man…in theory.

I was taking a massive leap of faith here, but I was all out of options, and I needed him to not see me as a threat, or he be so turned on that he didn't care that this situation made no sense. "You can check me first," I offered, trying not to seem as if I were affected by him right now because he looked unruffled. He didn't seem to care at all that I was partially naked, which didn't bode well for me. Damn, this plan makes no sense, and I don't know why he would go along with it other than curiosity, but I don't know what else to do.

He stood up, towering over me, and I tried not to flinch when his large hand came to my shoulder. He ran his fingers over my hair, pulling out the clip from my updo to shake out my curls. I assumed to look for a small weapon of sorts. Yet his fingers felt over my scalp gentler than expected, making my skin prickle in pleasure as I had to actively not lean into the caress of my scalp. His other hand inched unhurriedly down my back, sending a surge of want shivering down my spine, making my breathing hitch when he got to my ass. There was tension between us, but I did not know if it was just me who felt this attraction or him as well. If he feels it too, then this will be easier than predicted, especially since I want to open his shirt—at least one more button would be enough to satisfy me later when I think back to this moment. Staring at the small part of his chest so close to my face was torment, and I wanted to kiss it so much my lips burned.

I could feel his breath on my neck as he leaned to look around at my back, so I turned in his arms to give him a better look at my backside. I tried not to care when his hand pulled down my underwear to inspect me, and I could feel the heat of his eyes burning into my ass as he knelt down. He was so reserved I could hear a pin drop in the silence, and he was meticulous as he inspected any place I could hide a weapon. His strong hands pushed my legs apart as he opened my ass cheeks, making me hold my breath when I didn't expect him to do that. I blushed too much, and it was becoming impossible to hide my reaction when his fingertips grazed my opening. My skin burned in awareness from how close he was as he pulled back up my lingerie.

"Turn," he commanded, and when I did, he was still on his knees, looking over my body with narrowed eyes. "Noble women are normally much more timid," he murmured before sliding his rough hand up my stomach to cup my breast, pulling down my brassiere before he stood to examine me, and I held my breath from the anxiety of the situation. Oh God, he is so tall...

I focused on his open shirt as he checked my breasts for a weapon, hoping he couldn't feel how hard my heart was beating. "I have my reasons," I confessed, and I was shocked when he gave my breast a squeeze before pulling his hand back. I bit my lip, looking away as I felt more heat and tension take over me. I can't believe he has now seen every inch of me...why must this be so sensual? I am much too aroused right now.

"You have no weapon," he declared before sitting back down, and I nodded in agreement.

"I only came to learn one thing, and then I will leave. I would like to call it a personal query I have had that needs to be answered," I murmured seductively as I leaned forward to pull his tie off his neck, making sure to graze his face with my breast, and he followed the movement closely like I could still try to kill him. "I will only bind your hands at the front," I whispered as I knelt between his legs to restrain his wrists, and when I looked up, I saw a grin I didn't expect. His smug smile was shocking to the point the slightest breath could have blown me over.

"So, what do you want to know about me that needs my hands bound and you not fully dressed?" he questioned deviously, making me gulp. Maybe I don't need to test this theory if he is now acting like a cocky man.

"I will not pretend to assume you know about me, so I will explain..." I began, but he cut me off.

"Baroness Caroline Malta La'Blauvelt, no children, widow. Known for her understanding of the opposite sex, and all know of her skilled way with a pen," he stated as if he was reading a dossier on me. Yet I was shocked by his words, and his blue eyes burned into mine as if *he* were testing *me*.

"Well then, maybe you already guessed why I am here," I breathed as I undid his pants. "to seduce the man who is impenetrable," but there it was, my proof, hard as a rock bounding toward my face. Now, if I was wise, I would have just looked at it, dressed, and left. Told the king that his daughter's betrothed liked women; he just didn't trust people. I ***should*** have said that the princess would have to earn his trust before he would love her, but I am not smart because I leaned down, wanting him in my mouth. So I did what I desired, wetted my lips, and tasted him.

In fear that if I teased him, he wouldn't let me continue, I sucked him deep into my throat. His bound hands surprised me and went to my head, holding me in place; I missed that feeling of not thinking for a moment as I looked up to watch his face contort in pleasure. "Shit," he cursed, and it made my insides tighten in pride that I had gotten him on the first try—with honesty of all things. It spurred me on as I felt how tight his legs got beside my shoulders and how roughly he began to push up into my face. "God damn," he moaned as I cradled his balls and his fingers tugged at my scalp. Suddenly, a knock sounded at the door, and I went to pull back, but he held my head still, making me gag a bit. "No one is to enter this room until lunch tomorrow!" he thundered, his words surprising me.

"Yes, sir," the servant called before he let me move back up to breathe, and when I looked at him, I could see his face was red, with his head lulled back. He must have been close, and damn, was he especially attractive like this. No other aristocrat has been able to get this far before, so I wanted to ensure I finished this properly, at least for my reputation. I went back to pleasing him, his fingers fisting and tearing in my curls as I worked him with my mouth. I could feel his need with every pump into my throat and every groan that left his lips. This man was pent up; I could feel it, and I am pent up as well.

I rolled his balls around in my hand, taking him as far back as I could as I worked his shaft with my other hand. "Shit," he grunted loudly before I felt his cum in the back of my throat. He held my head steady, not allowing me to move, and I really liked that control he kept while even tied up...lucky princess.

When he released my hair, I leaned back on my heels to look over this man who now seemed relaxed, lying against the couch, clothes a mess. "I imagine that was better than me trying to kill you," I jested as I moved to stand on my wobbly legs.

"Fuck it," he growled as he easily tore the tie on his wrists, pulling me down onto his lap to kiss me. His tongue invaded my mouth, swirling powerfully as he controlled my head, not allowing me to move. My mind spun, and I had to mentally push myself off him before my body would follow.

"Ah, what are you doing?" I exclaimed as I shoved him away, but he held me, not letting me go.

"Was that really what you came for?" he breathed heavily, and I chuckled, leaning forward to kiss up his strong neck, wanting to take back some control for my sanity.

"I just wanted to see if the rumors were true. I can be too curious sometimes. Especially when it is all the other ladies can speak about. It will be exciting to be the only one to know the truth," I admitted as I licked up to his ear, and his fingers tightened on my spine before I felt him unlace my brassiere.

"I am not so sure that is enough," he hummed deeply as he lifted me and began to walk with ease toward a set of double doors. I talk a big game, but up until now, I had only pleasured my husband, so the second I saw the bed, my nerves kicked in. I was fine before because I was so in the moment, but now I am freaking out.

"I am not supposed to sleep with you. I just wanted to know. Ahhh," I yelled as he tossed me on the bed, and I held my brassiere so my breasts wouldn't slip out.

"Not supposed to sleep with me? Who gave you this order?" he scoffed as he began to disrobe, distracting me with his fit body built by the war.

"Ah, um. Look, I-I was only supposed to verify you like women, a-and I did that," I stammered, and he stopped to look at me with a dangerous grin from where I knelt on the bed I had never seen him make such a face before, and it was deviously seductive. It should be illegal!

"What a shame. It looks like you are about to get in trouble," he declared playfully as he came toward me. I rolled off the bed to the other side, and he chased after me.

"I swear I only came to..." I began but stopped when he strode closer, and I backed up until my ass hit the nightstand.

"Came to suck me off? You really want nothing more?" he questioned as he looked down at me like I was foolish before tearing my bra off, so I was now almost naked. I was losing my composure with how much I did not want to stop his pursuit of me...I really wanted to continue.

"Even if I want to, I shouldn't. You are promised to the princess," I proclaimed as he leaned into my body so I could feel his hardness on my leg, and he pushed his knee between my thighs to spread me apart. Making my whole being burn in anticipation. How did this get so out of control?

"I am promised to no one," he cursed as he leaned down, closing the distance, and claimed my lips. He was so shocking with how intense the kiss was, yet I didn't expect his hands to hover over my arms as if waiting for me to accept his offer. It has been over a year since I had sex, and every part of me ached to do it, especially after such a long build-up. Once should be fine, I reasoned. His tongue swirled in my mouth, and when I deepened it, pulling him into me, he took me in his arms, bringing me to the bed.

I learned two things about him this day. One, his appetite was impressive, and two, he was most certainly a lover of women. "You were wet when I searched you," he groaned against my neck as he began to kiss down my chest, pulling me into his erection by my ass to grind into me.

"You weren't supposed to notice," I moaned when he leaned his head down lower, sucking my nipple into his mouth, making me cry out.

"I notice quite a bit," he drawled as he pulled my underwear off, and his hardness brushed my opening. I expected him to slide in, but he pressed it between us, using it to massage my clit, and the pleasure it gave me was enough to make me beg if I wasn't careful. Just the way he looked at me was enough to make me melt into nothing. "You are much too loud for so many ears around," he chuckled as his hand moved to cover my mouth, and he slid in making me whimper into his hand from his size and quick intrusion. It has been so long that my whole body trembled from my building need. He groaned into my ear as he thrusted leisurely in me, and I got wetter from the angle, hitting right where I had missed for years.

"A-arrchdduke," I whined under his hand, but the words came out muffled, and he moved his hand to let me speak. "Archduke, right there, don't stop," I cried, and he covered my mouth again.

"If I let you moan, at least call me Claude," he breathed into my ear before rolling us over so I was sitting on him. He uncovered my mouth, and I rode him quickly as my orgasm grew, chasing that feeling I so longed for. I felt like fire was inside me, needing to escape, and I wanted to let it out. I bit my lip, relishing how he watched me so intensely, and I tried my hardest not to make a sound, but I was so close. I moved harder against him, and he reached up, cupping my breasts before squeezing them, bringing them into his mouth to suck on my nipples. The second his mouth licked my skin, I whimpered, unable to stop it as my hand slammed into the headboard, and I thrust on him wildly until my orgasm stopped, leaving me out of breath from moaning so loudly, crumbling forward on his chest. "It is like you wish to sully my reputation," he chuckled, rolling me to my back to pound into me. "No, one should hear what I am doing to you," he whispered against my shoulder before biting it.

I was too far gone at this point; I was the wettest I had ever been and just came unbelievably hard, so I lay there, letting him have his way. I had never known what it was like to be so tormented in bed, but this must be it. Body spent, but unwilling to stop. God, I don't want him to stop. It all feels like I could melt into him, and he fills me so completely. "Ugh, right there," I begged as I leaned up, hugging him, wrapping my legs around his hips to move with him. His mouth bit and sucked down my neck across to my shoulder, his fingers twisting and knotting in my hair until I cried out cumming again when he had covered my mouth, his fingers shoving down my throat, stealing my air to silence me.

After another moment, he pulled from me, and I felt warm liquid hit my stomach. He came with ragged breaths, but I was too wrapped up in my own pleasure to pay attention to him until I felt something cool and wet rub over my skin. "What is that?" I grumbled as I opened one eye to look, seeing that he was cleaning me off.

"A towel," he spoke with no emotion before throwing it on the floor and getting in the bed. I rolled over, letting him in, but I had no idea what the protocol was for this. I have never had a one-night stand, and not many other upper-class women do either, so I have zero experience here.

"Oh, thank you. I only need a moment, and then I can get ready to leave," I said as I nestled into the soft bed, really not wanting to leave this euphoric peace yet.

"We aren't done," he announced, and I turned to my other side to look at him. I narrowed my eyes at his tight jawline, and he looked upset again, which bothered me. Did I not do good enough, so he isn't satisfied?

"Fine, but I need to send a letter to my maid, and I want something to eat," I demanded, and he looked at me for a moment, then grinned. Every time he did, it was so shocking that it made me feel my neck to ensure it was still attached and I wasn't dead. But he did as I asked, getting me a pen and stationary before leaving the room to, I assume, get food. So I pulled on his jacket, since he was wearing his shirt, and went to sit at the large desk in the corner.

How do I tell Janet I succeeded and to send my victory letter to the king tonight so this can all be done with by morning? She is smart, she knows me. I just need to be vague in case he reads it.

Dear Janet,

Do not be concerned for my absence this evening. The archduke, in his graciousness, wished to show me a book in his library, but alas, upon our arrival, I fear I may have consumed something at the track that didnt agree with me. Worry not; the attentive staff here are ensuring my comfort and care. You would be proud of how I am being handeled.

I shall return by morning. Kindly gather all my correspondence to bring along to the tea party, lest I miss the post. There are very important letters that must be sent out as soon as possible, so please double-check your work. See you in the morning, and don't stay up worrying about me.

Madam La Blauvelt

Janet should understand that perfectly.

4

A Torture of the Tongue

When the archduke walked back in, he stopped to look at me from where I sat at his desk in only his jacket. His reaction was what I had hoped—stunned, yearning was all over his face. "Here, you might as well read it yourself instead of your staff telling you later," I offered, holding out the letter for Janet as he set down the large plate of pasta in front of me, taking the paper to read. However, I was more excited about the fantastic food before me than his reaction to what I wrote.

"You are here from a sickness, and it's okay because of books?" he questioned arrogantly, and his critique was irritating.

"Too much, icecream" I hummed before taking the fork, swirling the noodles to eat a large bite of the creamy, white sauced noodles, "but I very well can't say I seduced the archduke, and for some reason, he wants me to stay over, now can I?" I teased through my full mouth, letting out a happy groan from the taste of the food.

"You did not seduce me. I would have had you at some point," he declared, looking offended before walking to the door to hand the letter to someone. "Have this delivered as soon as possible," he instructed, and I was shocked by his words because I didn't actually believe that he would do that.

"Don't take away my victory. I got you, not the other way around," I reprimanded him, making him grin at me again to the point where I almost believed he thought this was all him.

I took another large bite of the creamy pasta and wiggled in happiness, making the jacket shift down my shoulders, and I allowed it in hopes he would enjoy the show. I could feel his eyes burning into me, and being under his gaze made my whole body feel hot. "You can fit a lot in that mouth," he declared, and I looked back at him smugly.

"Thankfully, you have a lot to give," I hummed before pushing the plate away. "Now, what do you wish to do? Since you are making me stay," I lilted as I pulled open the jacket to reveal more of my body to him. I know men love women in their clothes, and he seems no different with how he is watching me.

"Torture you for the truth," he grinned, making his eyes shine brighter, and I nodded nonchalantly, trying to seem unaffected by his searing gaze.

"Torment me all you wish, but I will like it more than you think," I crooned, smiling at him. His usual cold eyes seemed softer.

"By the end of this night, I will know who commissioned you and why a short, overweight man was following me," he declared. It wasn't shocking that he knew he was being tailed, it is not as if the king's minion was stealthy, and he blended in poorly. I just hated that he thought I chose that man to follow him, not forced to tolerate him by the king.

"If it helps, I really do like children and the races," I flirted as I dropped the jacket, and his eyes narrowed with desire.

"So, you admit you have a benefactor. This wasn't solely for you?" he questioned as he took off his shirt before walking over to cup my face, gentler than I expected.

"Where is this torture you promised? Because I know how to keep a secret," I hummed, and he shook his head in irritation. His hand slid to my neck, gripping it tightly, pulling my mouth to his.

"If you tell anyone about this, I will kill you," he threatened, his words a breath over my lips, and I giggled at this lousy situation.

"Then I guess I am a dead woman," I whispered sarcastically, and he looked at me with that unreadable glare I didn't understand as his hands slid to my arms, tightening to the point it was painful. "If it helps, the person wouldn't want others to know. So, your secret is safe," I breathed, trying not to wince as his fingers dug into my skin. I shouldn't have admitted I had already notified someone in the letter he just sent. A knot sat in me in fear that he might actually kill me. He had already pulled a sword on me once; it wouldn't be so hard again.

"I can have this person killed. You should be more scared right now. I am very displeased," he gritted his teeth, and I winced as his fingers dug deeper into my arms, making me actually afraid.

"You can't. They are above your reach," I admitted, trying not to show any fear because I didn't think he would kill me like this. At least not while I am naked...one could hope.

"Above my reach. No one is above my..." he laughed cruelly but stopped as if he had an epiphany. "It's the king. The king made you do this," he crooned darkly.

I whimpered from the pain of his grasp, and he pulled his hands off me. "I should go," I whispered, unable to meet his eyes as I stepped around him to find my dress. Suddenly terrified that he was upset enough to torture me.

He followed close behind, and my skin prickled in anxiety that he wouldn't let me leave this place after what we had done. "I don't believe that you wanted to do this with me, especially after the last time we met. You must be disgusted having to bed a man you detest," he snapped, and I tilted my head to look at his enraged face. His blue eyes burned to the point I knew I needed to calm him, or I wouldn't leave here unharmed.

"I don't detest you. Honestly, I understand you. We both are mercenaries in different ways. This was just the first time I willingly gave another man my body besides my husband,"

I confessed as a weird guilt swirled in me like I had cheated on Ronald. "as I said before, I wanted to seduce you. There were other ways to get proof besides tying you up to pleasure you," I muttered as I walked to pull on my dress, opting to leave my undergarments in the urgency to get out. "I didn't lie when I said I wanted to, but I should go before I make this worse," I tried to explain, hoping he would take pity on me.

"Let me see your arms," he commanded, and I looked back at him in surprise as I stilled my trembling fingers on the buttons of my dress.

"Don't worry about it. I merely bruise easily," I whispered, feeling too embarrassed to meet his eyes.

"Let me see you," he demanded slowly as he watched me cautiously like *I* could somehow kill him.

I walked back over to him, and his eyes softened as he looked over the finger marks on my upper arms. When he reached out, I allowed myself to flinch, hoping he felt guilty about what he had done. "Stay," he requested calmly as he looked down into my eyes. I was so confused by his mood swings that I didn't know how to proceed.

"I think me being here will only upset you further, and I am much smaller than you," I whispered as I stepped back, hoping I made my point because I foolishly wanted to stay.

"Yes, you are very small," he agreed before stepping closer to me, sucking all the air from my chest. His hand reached out to undo the buttons I had done, and his eyes never left mine as he pushed the dress off my shoulders. "Only your husband and I have had you?" he questioned, watching me closely, making a strange tingle pulse in my body.

"And myself," I laughed quietly, hoping it would break the tension in the room, and he chuckled before leaning down to kiss the marks on my arms from him. He was so gentle that it melted the anxiety in me as I was lost in the darkness of him, holding on to this spark of pleasure with him.

"Stay," he whispered as he kissed across my chest to my other arm, and I felt drawn to the heat in him. "I won't hurt you ever again," he declared as he kissed each finger imprint on my arm. I gazed over his bare shoulder at the vast room, contemplating whether this was wise. It didn't feel smart to get involved with him like this, especially with his temper, but even if he didn't say he was sorry, he looked it.

"Don't make promises you can't keep Archduke Sigmund," I whispered before running my fingers through his perfect blond hair, and he knelt in front of me, kissing down my chest. He moved lower, and I was shocked when he kissed my sex, teasing me open with his tongue.

"Mmm, so sweet," he rasped as I knotted my fingers in his hair to steady myself. Just the slightest touches were enough to make me forget about what just happened as he knelt before me, pleasing me. The archduke, who was frigid to all, was kneeling before me, pleasuring me beyond belief, and it was empowering.

He focused on my clit, licking and sucking fiercely to the point I had never felt so much pleasure for so long. "You are so wet," he groaned against my mound, holding me tightly to his face by my ass. So I ground against his face because he seemed to want me to as he moved me, his fingers kneading and groping my ass. He suddenly stood, lifting me to set me down on his desk before going right back to it. I fell back in my pleasure, unable to stay up straight as he spread me apart with his fingers, concentrating right where I needed.

"Please, Claude, please...I...I am..." I whimpered, shaking uncontrollably as he moved back, rubbing his fingers over me quickly, and I felt a rush of relief with the largest and longest orgasm I had ever felt crash down on me from his skilled build-up. I couldn't comprehend what had happened before he rolled me over and slid back into me, pounding me with an intensity that made the whole desk move.

"Fuck, you are so lovely," he cursed as his finger came up to interlace with mine, knotting us together as he bit across my back. He slowed his pace, pulling me to my hands and knees before he moved in me unhurriedly from behind. He curved his body over mine, turning and sucking my breast roughly into his mouth, making me cry out into the room. "Shh, little spy," he groaned as his mouth left my breast to bite my neck, his tongue teasing over my lips before he bit the corner of my mouth.

"Claude," I cried against his lips, overwhelmed by all the sensations as his body completely covered my back.

"So lovely," he echoed before he pulled out, and I felt warmth hit my backside.

We both had come again, and every bit of me wanted to sleep even as I felt him cleaning me up and taking me to bed. I could barely keep my eyes open after cumming so hard that I was exhausted. "We were much too loud," he remarked. I nodded in sleepy agreement as he lay me in the bed, his hand caressing my back. "You also bruise much too easily," he groaned before I felt him slide into bed behind me.

"I probably do not eat enough meat," I grumbled, and he chuckled.

"You are a surprisingly funny woman," he admitted as it took everything in me to stay awake.

"You are much more giving than I imagined," I teased as I turned to face him. He looked at me seriously. Why was he so serious after what we had just done? "Do you ever relax?" I asked as I pushed his tousled hair back from his face, noticing an inch-long, silver scar in his hairline—probably from the war.

"Not often do I have the luxury," he said as he observed me.

"I see. Well, I will go to sleep first, so you do not think I will try to kill you in your dreams, or I can go to the couch," I poked, making him grin at me before pulling me into his chest. I was shocked to feel his erection pressed between us. How can he be hard again?

"I am not done with you," he breathed over my lips before kissing me slowly and passionately until his hands had caressed every inch of me until he pushed back into me. "You have the best pussy I have ever felt," he rasped as he pulled my leg over his hip, taking his time, and I liked it too much.

"So damn tight and wet," he cursed against my lips as his fingers laced with mine, and he rolled me to my back fucking me slowly. Giving me pleasure I had only dreamed could exist, and I was going to miss this after tonight. I had never experienced anything like this before, as if I could feel every touch over every nerve. His hands left not one part of me untouched as his fingers wove into the hair at the base of my neck to tug my head back, his teeth and tongue trailing my skin, and all I could do was moan as I wrapped my legs over his hips to match the intensity. My skin became hot and clammy, the heat in the room almost suffocating in the best of ways. It also didn't feel real how my body yielded, and I came trembling under him so quickly it was almost embarrassing. I could feel his lips curl into a grin against my cheek before he pulled out to cum on my stomach, and I have no recollection of what he did after as I fell right to sleep in the middle of the bed, uncaring if I was now unclean.

It had to have been late or very, very early as I awoke to him kissing along my shoulder, his throbbing cock pressed against my ass. The idea he wanted more of me was dangerous for my ego, so I turned in his arms, and I could feel just about every pulse with my body still humming from the ravaging he gave me not long ago. "I was asleep," I whisper, my face tucking against his neck where I sucked softly. The taste of salt from our earlier effort gave me a boost of pride, and with only low melted candles light left, the mood changed in a way I hadn't felt in years that was slightly terrifying.

"I wasn't," he hummed a line down my cheek to my neck that slightly ached from his unrelenting lips. "Open your legs wider," I followed his command as he hauled me up to his lap, where he knelt on the bed. His eyes never left mine as he slid inside, and my head fell back from the pleasure. He cradled me in his arms as we rocked, my nails digging into his back until I couldn't take the slow torment anymore. His gaze was unrelenting, and I had never had a man look at me in such a possessing way before as if he wanted to watch my pleasure—like that's all that mattered to him. It made me want to show him just how much I enjoyed this; I threw my head to grind against him quickly. "I wish I could scream," I admitted, and he leaned me back so my back arched off as I used my head on the bed for support. He slammed into me harder, his fingers digging into my hips as I could no longer control myself. "You make me scream," I whimpered, and the way he used me, moving like I was nothing, was something only I had done in dreams.

"Fucking ride, me," he ordered, and I rolled my hips up to match him, my breasts bouncing with every thrust. I was so close when he slowed, leaning forward, lifting me just enough he could switch before pinning me to the bed. "I'll cum if you do that," he cursed, his teeth grating against my nipple.

I curled against him, lifting my leg to push into him, needing that release, "Don't stop," I implored, feeling it about to break, "Harder," I begged as I swirled my tongue in his ear.

"Fuck," he cursed as I began to shake, my teeth sinking into his shoulder, whimpering as I came. It was too much to bear as her body arched, toes curling, legs so strained I feared it would push him out from between my legs. Not a second after I finished, I felt his cum hit me once more, but I was too exhausted to care as I curled into a ball, pulled the sheet over myself, and fell into a dreamless pleasure-induced sleep.

That night, I gave in to the archduke and allowed him to have me all night until we both could no longer keep our eyes open, and I knew that nothing would ever top this...

5

Quite the Opposite

I awoke before him the following day because I was hot with him wrapped around me so tightly. I felt like I was dying of heat exhaustion, with how sweaty and sticky I was from last night. I rolled my lower body out of bed slowly so his leg slid off me without waking him, though moving his arm over my chest was harder as I slid down the mattress so my face was pressed into his bare chest to slide out all the way. It was a struggle not to stare at his chest in desire and wish to stay to cum one more time, but I needed to get out before he woke. So I crept around the room gathering all my things, leaving my underwear in my haste or as a present before escaping to the other room with the desk to dress quickly.

As I finished my buttons, I looked at the desk in satisfaction, seeing that it had moved at least two feet from where it was before. Claude was such an unrelenting man, a beast in bed. I am going to miss that. God, the princess will be fortunate.

I piled my hair on top of my head and held my shoes in my hand as I snuck out of the door into the massive hall. I almost forgot how important this man was, but he lives in a castle by himself.

Once further down the rambling hall, I put on my shoes so the sounds wouldn't echo and made my way back the way he had brought me here, but this place is so enormous I don't know why he was worried about people hearing us. If we had done this in my townhouse, the whole city would have heard us, and he is by no means quiet either. For being so expressionless, he was so very different in bed. I held my cheeks as I felt them redden at the image of him groaning as he pushed into me. He really was a beast. The princess has no idea how good she is about to have it, I thought just as I snuck out a small door that led to the stables. I saw his coach and followed the road out to the front entry. Only a gardener up so early to see me, but he paid me no mind as he continued to trim up a low set of purple shrubs.

I walked under the gigantic oak tree canopy, soothed by the cool breeze on my sticky skin. Something about this driveway was magical; you could see nothing but the sun streaming through the leaves. I would love to go on walks here again; perhaps the princess will invite me as a thank you, I thought cynically. When I stepped out onto the main street, I was hoping that a taxi carriage would be free early in the morning, but everyone seemed to be still asleep. I had only slept maybe an hour or two because Claude played with me most of the night.

"*Wonderful, now I have to walk,*" I groaned, feeling like a limp bean after last night. If I hadn't already RSVP'd to the tea party today, I would stay in bed all day to recover and daydream of last night. I have never had so much fantastic sex in one night nor cum so many times; I pondered as I made my way toward my townhouse. Mercifully, my thoughts were interrupted when I heard horse hooves clomping, and I turned to see the milkman going by. I waved him down, and he slowed to look me over curiously. "My carriage broke down, and I am on my way back from a party. Could you please give me a ride home so I do not have to wait for my coachman? It is a rather brisk morning," I requested sweetly, batting my eyes, and he smiled at me before letting me on. He thankfully didn't question my story like a noble carriage man would; I suppose he has seen worse in his old age. But I was just thankful for the quiet ride beside him to the house because I knew Janet would not leave me alone the second I got home.

Alas, I somehow avoided Janet all the way up until my bath, when she barged in just as I sank into the cool water to soothe my sore, exceptionally dirty body. "Madam! How could you not have come straight for me!? I need to know what happened," she scolded me, and I sunk lower in the water to hide the hickeys on my body.

"You should know. I sent a letter," I said, and she looked at me in confusion.

"It only said that you would be home in the morning since Archduke Sigmund was holding you for questioning," she voiced nervously as she came to look me over carefully. She was worried about me; I could see it in her eyes.

"Indeed, he would never send my letter. How I despise his cleverness," I lamented, submerging myself beneath the water to wash away the guilt that accompanied my unexpected joy at Janet's inability to reveal my secrets to the king. I am not ready to let anyone else know about him yet. Maybe we can have just a little more time to play.

When I came back up, Janet looked over my naked body in the water with fearful eyes. She seemed on the verge of tears as she sank beside me to hold my face in her trembling hands. "Did that evil man torture you?!" she cried, her eyes landing on my arms, which did have relatively large bruises on my soft skin. That and hickeys trailed down my chest to the inside of my thighs.

"No, quite the opposite, actually. Janet, no one can know I spent the night with the archduke. He will kill anyone who knows what we did," I admitted, needing to ensure she stayed safe.

"What you did?" she murmured, and I hid my grin under the water.

"The archduke is a very giving man, so I do not plan to ruin his generosity," I mused, suddenly lost in the thought of how he had made me cum on his face so skillfully. He really knew what women liked, and I can't believe anyone never noticed that in his cocky stride. We were all idiots to worry about him. I wonder if he will call on me again.

"Mistress, you look pleased," Janet stated, and I looked back at her with a soft smile.

"Yes, it has been a while since I felt so good," I admitted. When I got out of the water, she examined my body in shock.

"Perhaps you will have to wear the lace dress...if only it were winter, we could hide these with long sleeves and a high neck," she complained anxiously. I was worried about how to hide the evidence of last night, but I was more worried about whether my legs could hold me up all day. After last night, I will have to sit for most of the day.

Janet did her best to cover the marks on my arms with concealer, yet my neck still had red marks all over that looked like a rash once the makeup was on. Thankfully, I could hide some with my hair, so I just need to not draw too much attention to myself today, and all will be fine. But that was proving to be an issue because it seemed that the king had told the princess of the plan for me to seduce the archduke. I only assumed that, by the way, her eyes shot daggers at me from across the tea table, and she didn't let me out of her sight for even a moment. This might have been the worst mistake of my career if anyone were to find out I stabbed the princess in the back as a mere baron's widow.

6

A Proposition from the Archduke

I had planned to leave the tea quickly, especially after the princess openly glared and sniped at me. Asking me pointed questions and ignoring my answers, I almost wished she would just come out and ask me about the archduke. Not that I would tell her, but it would be better than this animosity that the other ladies were picking up on. I wasn't scared of '*her*' because what mattered most was what her father wanted, and I was frankly jealous that she got to have the archduke as her husband one day. He was going to make her cum all the time, and honestly, it was bothersome to picture. In my exhausted state, my imagination was running rampant, and I was irritated by the princess's scowling at me when she should look smug. "I hear that your dresses for summer were bought from last season's collection," Princess

Flora sang, and I had to stifle an eye roll before sipping my tea.

"Did you not hear her?" Lady Gloria cracked, and I turned to look back at them, pretending to be oblivious.

"I thought she was talking to you. Because you wore that dress a few parties ago," I mused, letting my petty side show more than I should have, but I was exhausted. The room suddenly quieted, with the princess's eyes growing wide. I turned to see why all the ladies had stopped talking, and I swallowed hard as the archduke and crown prince walked into the room. "Damn," I cursed under my breath. Why is he here? He never comes to any social events unless coerced by the king. Even then, he doesn't always come. The crown prince consistently stops by to flirt with the ladies and to see his betrothed, but never with the archduke.

I set down my teacup and brought my fan up to my chest to hide my fluster from the other ladies, who all were thankfully busy drooling over the men. I don't know why I am so nervous right now, but my whole body feels as if it is ablaze, as if he is still touching me. "Ladies," the crown prince offered as a greeting, and prickles ran down my back when I felt the presence of the archduke behind me. I was so flustered by the feeling of his presence that I didn't greet the prince when all the other ladies at my table had.

I didn't need to look to know it was the archduke who stood behind me. The way the princess beamed at him was proof enough of who it was. "It is warm, Archduke Sigmund. How have you been enjoying the summer in the city?" Princes Flora asked, and I had to bite back a grin, trying not to chuckle at her poor attempt at conversation, which thankfully broke my tension...always the weather with ladies.

"It was rather searing last night, but I found it exceptionally cold this morning when I awoke," he remarked, and I straightened my spine at his words—were they pointed at me?

"I hope you do find a way to stay cool," the princess swooned, and suddenly, I felt his hand run up the side of my back, making my whole body constrict in desire. Every place he touched turned molten in want from the secret of his caress.

"I hope to enjoy the heat more. Wouldn't you agree, Madam La'Blauvelt?" the archduke asked me as I fanned myself. I turned to look up at his indifferent face, yet his fingers did not stop moving slow circles on my back, hidden from view.

"I would be wary of how much time you spend in the *heat*. You could get *burned*," I teased, watching as the corner of his lip pulled up a touch, but he never lost his calm demeanor. The princess cleared her throat, pulling my eyes back to her when I realized I had been staring up at him for far too long.

"You should take your own advice. Your maids seem to be having a difficult time covering your sunburns," Princess Flora retorted, and I exhaled in relief that she was too naive to know what these marks really were.

"It is rather unsightly," Lady Gloria sniggered as she and the princess grinned at each other.

"Sunburns, let me see," the crown prince commanded from where he had been watching his sister try to flirt before belittling me. With amusement in his blue eyes, he pushed my fan down, looking over my breasts greedily, and I couldn't push him away. The archduke's finger stilled on my back before he put his arm out in front of me, blocking the prince's ogling.

"She does not need more eyes unless it's a doctor's," the archduke snapped, and I felt as if I was in the middle of something I shouldn't be.

"No harm, no foul. Prince, please take my seat. I was just about to move about the room. I was feeling bored with this table's conversation," I offered. Though, I was not annoyed by the prince in the least for leering. He had done many more inappropriate things to me before; his staring was harmless.

Thankfully, the prince accepted my seat, giving me an out from Princess Flora's searching eyes, and to get away before the prince said something more improper and the princess insulted me further. As I walked past Claude, I felt the tension in me again as our eyes met, and I swear I saw a smile behind them. This was fun, being the only one to know he likes women, and having bedded the man all these ladies dream of was like a seductive tease.

I walked *far* away to the other side of the large solarium to get a tea sandwich but jumped when I felt pressure on my ass. "Jeez," I choked, almost dropping my food.

"Why did you leave without saying goodbye? You didn't even take a carriage," the archduke whispered, and I was shocked by how close he was standing to me with so many others around. My back was practically pressed to his chest, and my lust was suddenly unbearable as he was so close.

"Why are you here?" I spoke in hushed tones.

"Because it is where you are," he noted, and I turned to look up at him, narrowing my eyes. I don't trust this or the butterflies his words gave me. Hearing him chuckle so deeply made me shift my legs tighter together. God, he is so alluring.

"I left early so as not to bother you, and the nice milkman gave me a ride," I quipped, and his eyes narrowed back at me.

"I was planning to let you leave. You were not a captive," he murmured, and I grinned at his pinch brow. He looked upset, and I rather liked it until I felt his free hand graze my wrist.

"Are you sure?" I teased as I took a bite of the small sandwich to hide my fluster from the touch, and he eyed my mouth. "My maid's note said otherwise,"

"I had planned to have you at least once more before feeding you and escorting you home," he declared as if offended, but his finger slid down the pulse point of my wrist until his fingers caressed my palm. He was maddening.

"Have me?" I was losing my composer as my body hummed from the touch and the intensity of his gaze. "You think highly..." I began but stopped as he stood up straighter, taking my glove with him. Surprisingly, he didn't move away from me as the crown prince came to lean against the food table to the side of us. I could only clench my hand from the burning his touch left.

"I didn't even notice she was here hidden in front of you," the prince crooned, and even with that remark, the archduke didn't take a step out of my space. "Was he pestering you for an autograph? All his men would be jealous if he got one," the crown prince remarked as he looked over the assortment of cookies in delight.

"An autograph? Because of my advice service?" I asked as I turned to look at the archduke, and he stared back at me in the most confusing way, like he was watching me for a mistake.

"Yes, the single men all write to you while deployed. You are quite the celebrity to the military men, but you must know that," the crown prince explained as he settled on a small raspberry cookie, then turned to look back at us with a grin.

"I would be more than happy to schedule a time to visit the injured men and give autographs. However, the archduke doesn't seem like the type of man to care about something so fanciful as what I do for a living," I offered, and the prince leaned in toward me to the point I wanted to lean back but held my ground as the archduke touched my lower back, startling me—I was stuck between them.

"Well, if you *came*, it would *please* all the men," the prince whispered suggestively, and I felt the archduke's hand on my back tighten.

"That is enough. Go check on your betrothed," the archduke snapped. I was shocked by the archduke's discourtesy toward the crown prince, but the prince didn't seem to notice as he sauntered off, eating his treat.

"So you wrote to me?" I flirted as I turned towards him, and he stared down at me in frustration or anger—I wasn't quite sure.

"I did not, but my men still do," he admitted as he took his hand off me, and I noted the loss of the touch.

"I see. Well, perhaps you can write to me about your growing issue with your future father-in-law since somehow he was not informed of something important last night...making me a liar and look bad at my job," I snipped. He grinned fully, making my insides tighten in yearning—he had me completely in a knot.

"I do not plan to marry the princess, so I do not care about this issue, but just you talking to me privately for this long will get back to the king, so your reputation will be intact," he whispered as he stepped more into my space, and I refused to back down. With him so close, I wanted to kiss him, but what he was doing was so out of character that I didn't know what to do.

"You are a confusing man," I breathed. His eyes looked over me again before his hand moved toward me but stopped so close to my face that I was drawn to the sensation it created in me.

"I am ashamed of your arms. I could see the bruises when I first came in," he said apologetically as he reached for my other glove. The fabric easily slipped past my fingertips, and I stepped back in shock. What is going on?!

"Archduke..." I began, but he took another step closer as he pocketed my gloves, leaving me nowhere to move.

"I told you to call me Claude," he smirked, and I bit my lip as my longing to kiss him grew. I wanted to be alone with him again because, somehow, last night wasn't enough.

"You are about to ruin your reputation if you don't take a step back," I whispered, and when I looked around his back, I could see no less than eight women, including the princess, watching me with pure hatred.

"I think it will be fine, considering I have a business proposal for you," he declared as I looked back up at him.

"All business meetings are held between three and six at *my* estate," I hummed while moving away, "You are more than welcome to talk to me then, but for now, just enjoy the tea," I teased before walking away toward Janet, who waited in the hall outside of the main room. She had a tight-lined smile that made me grin at how pleased she looked, and I had to hide how happy I was that the archduke came to the tea just to see me. My now bare fingers were a clear provocation that he also enjoyed our time together.

We sauntered out to the carriages, and I was satisfied leaving after giving them my two hours and the archduke my two gloves. "Mistress, he watched you walk away until you were out of sight," Janet exclaimed. I had to admit I was unbelievably hot and bothered by our conversation, but I had to leave him wanting more, or he might not show up later...if he got my meaning. "oh, let me go back for your gloves," she noted, turning to leave, but I clung to her arm with a wicked smile playing on my face.

"You will not find them," I hummed as the carriages came into view. "not unless you take up pickpocketing as a hobby," and I didn't need to say anymore because Janet understood perfectly by the satisfied grin that grew on her face.

Three o'clock came, and I had expected him to show up, but nothing. If I had known he wasn't going to come over, I would have napped longer.

Four o'clock came, and nothing. It gave me time to write to all the people who needed advice, but that was not what I wished to be doing right now.

At five o'clock, I was growing upset that I had wasted my day agonizing over a man instead of catching up on sleep. I had reset my hair and even washed up again just to make sure I smelled good everywhere, even applying my honey body powder.

By *six o'clock*, I had had dinner and given up hope he would come, so I settled on keeping my mind off him by reading in the study. I don't know what I expected; he is only now showing interest in a woman, and it's possible that I was more taken than he was. Honestly, I might need to stay away if I am already so hung up on him.

I sat with a huff pulling out a book I had read a million times but couldn't get into it when all I could think about were Claude's cold blue eyes warming when he smiled at me or how it felt to cum on his face. Ugh, it is not like I am a love-sick teen, but I can not focus on anything other than his touch—I groaned as I leaned forward into the book. "You have poor security," I heard from the open window right before the archduke came crawling in, startling me.

"Ah," I screeched, holding my chest. "Jeez. Is that necessary?" I exclaimed, but in the back of my mind, I thought of how sexy it was.

"Well, I plan to stay past business hours, so yes," he grinned as he stalked toward me, and his size was extremely intimidating in a good way.

"Let's start with business," I managed to say with an air of nonchalance as I motioned for him to take a seat across from me on the couch. Which he reluctantly did.

"Then I would like to get this part over with quickly," he declared as he loosened his tie. He must know how sexy that was and is tormenting me.

I leaned over to fill two tumblers with brown liquor before handing him one, setting the bottle between us on the tea table. "Before I agree to anything, you must answer all my questions. If you can't, you take a shot," I instructed, and he nodded yes before chuckling.

"The same for you. Nothing is off limits, and you can not lie," he countered, which was unexpected.

"Fine, but you go first with your proposition," I instructed, and he watched me closely for a while as I shifted to get comfortable in the armchair.

"Did you wear that for me?" he asked, and I grinned, but that question was not what he was supposed to start with.

"No, I wear it for me. Silk is nice in the summer; it helps with the *heat*," I teased like our joke from earlier, and he looked over me in appreciation in my thin black night dress. I relaxed back so he could get a good view, and I was tempted to uncross my legs so he could see just how ready I had been all day. "What is your proposition?" I asked again, pulling his eyes from my body.

"I need blackmail on four men, enough to legally have rights to kill them with the littlest of pushback possible. Since I was gone for so long on the battlefield, I am behind on any information," he explained, and I nodded, taking a sip because I did not like where this was going.

"As I said before, I have only slept with you and my husband. I will not use my body as a way to help you," I scoffed, and his eyes darkened somehow.

"That is not what I asked for," he snapped before taking a long drink. Maybe we both don't understand the rules of this game. "I simply want your experience in social circles for private investigation. Your body will stay as is," he said gruffly, and I nodded in understanding. "I believe I shall start now that business was discussed," he continued, and I nodded along, waiting for his question.

Depending on the men, what he was asking from me didn't seem too hard. I might already know something. "How did you figure out this career as a noblewoman?" he asked, and that seemed like a very long conversation, not suitable for this atmosphere, but I could do my best to answer.

"Ronald, as you know, passed away from a weak constitution, and I won't lie and say it was a marriage of love. It was very much convenient. He was older, kind, and treated me as a friend, which was more than I could have ever hoped for. I learned quickly that if you do not love so deeply, it is easy to learn 'the hows and whys' of a relationship. Without so many strong emotions, I got to test out my ideas on him, and often, they were proven true. He told me to continue to write to the soldiers to offer companionship, and he also allowed me to publish in the paper. Without Ronald, I wouldn't have anything," I voiced fondly because Ronald was a good man. "Since we were unable to have an heir before he passed, I lost everything when his cousin seized control of the estate. So I have my title, but I am no more than working-class since I had such a small dowry," I admitted, and he took another long drink before setting down his empty glass.

"Do others know of this?" he asked, and it wasn't his turn, but I'd answer.

"For the past year, I have been able to hide it under the pretense of grief," I offered as I took a sip, now realizing the game was useless as we continued to sip our drink. We were only playing along under the front of learning about each other. But since the archduke came here and not my husband's family's estate, he must know something about it, or he wouldn't have found me. But I want to know more about the men he wants me to research first. That question of knowing about my circumstances can wait. "Who are the men?" I asked, and he looked around my small study as if sizing up the things I had after being forced out.

"John Pultas, Gulter Vandal, Halad Lasum, and Chal La'Blauvelt," when he said the last name, my hand trembled, and I gripped the chair for stability. Chal took my home and gave me nothing after trying to attack me.

"I would like to be there when he dies," I declared, and the archduke leaned in to look over my face, knowing the man I meant.

"Then give me a good reason to kill him," he spoke calmly, and I felt a strong sense of urgency to get to work.

7

The Value of Secrets

For the life of me, I can not figure out why I am not more scared of the archduke. He has threatened me more than once, and I know he could kill me, but something in the gentleness in his eyes makes me trust him. "What did Chal do to make you hate him so? You had no heir, so it was within legal rights to seize the estate," he asked, and I sighed, not wanting to answer that, so I took a long drink of alcohol.

"Use your imagination, what a man might try if rejected," I muttered before setting down the glass, and I watched his jaw tighten before knocking back his drink. I moved to refill it, and the tension in the room was no longer sexual as we danced around this topic, which was irritating. "Why those men?" I asked, and he looked at his drink for a long time. Maybe he wishes not to tell me.

"They all sent assassins of a sort to kill me. Halad almost succeeded," he explained, and I nodded in understanding. I imagine that, with the amount of power the archduke holds between the new and old governments, his life could be a precarious road to walk. "If you knew your husband was likely to die, why did you not try to have an heir?" he questioned, and I chuckled at how unabashedly intrusive he was.

"It was not from lack of trying. Of all things, Ronald was a very attentive partner. That was possibly the only thing we had in common. Not many forced into a marriage of convenience gets to enjoy themselves as much as I did," I admitted, and he cocked his eye at me before grinning, and suddenly that heat was back.

"I see, so that is why you are so forthcoming in bed. You are the best I have had," he complimented me, and I didn't want to tell him the same because that would be unfair to Ronald, who did well even with his weak constitution.

"For a man so well versed in a woman's body, why do you hide your desires?" I asked, and he took a long drink to the point I figured he wouldn't answer. That was the rule: if you didn't want to tell, you could just drink, but we both had been drinking anyway.

"Do you remember Miss Lasum? Halad's Younger sister? She was close to your age, maybe a year older," he questioned, and I nodded before looking at my glass, feeling as if I would need a drink after how serious his face just got because I know Miss Lasum, Rose, is dead. "Halad was intent on marrying her off to me before I went to war. I assumed at the time he hoped that in the event I died, my title would now be linked to his family. At the time, I turned him down because I liked another, and the promise of marrying the princess was also just announced, so I wasn't sure yet which route to take," he explained as if lost in deep thought, and the idea all this was going on during the war was not shocking. However, what was shocking was that he, at one point, considered the princess for marriage with how little he regarded her now. "When I turned his proposal down, he showed up at the front with her, and all was well until one night she snuck into my bed, and I was too naive at the time to understand it was a trap. Halad caught us and tried to make me take responsibility for my actions, but I refused, saying no one but us would know since it was only kissing. It was not worth marrying over when I didn't even know her," he explained, and a bit of guilt settled in me that I had done a similar thing to him, but at least I didn't want anything from him. Well, besides sex, that is what I want. "Halad pulled his gun, and in the struggle, it went off, and he shot his sister. So you understand now why I keep my affairs far from the capital and very private," he stated. I rubbed my face, feeling it flush from the heat of the drink and the story. Poor Rose, stuck in the middle of her brother's aspirations. "No one else knows that story besides Halad and me, so if it gets around, I know who said something. Just a warning," he remarked, and I nodded before drinking my whole glass. This was much more serious than I had expected this talk to be. But now I understand why he pulled his sword on me that first time we spoke. He had just watched a young woman die because of her brother's greed.

"I understand and value privacy," I declared before setting the glass down, knowing my limit was two, but he leaned forward to pour me another. I took it, looking over the dark liquid before taking a small sip.

"I like that about you," he drawled, and his compliment shocked me, but I smiled back at him, waiting for his question. He looked at me with a smirk that excited me that we were going to get back to the topic I wanted most, the reason I put honey powder all over my body. "If the king truly is the one who asked you to seek me out, why did you accept? Unless you had no choice," he asked directly this time, and since he already knew there was no reason to lie, especially with the lust in his eyes.

"I am probably too curious for my own good. I really did just want to see you naked, and it had been so long," I admitted. He leaned forward with a smug grin, and I shifted so I lay sideways in the chair, getting more comfortable in my drunken state.

"How can I be upset with that answer, considering I have wanted to see you naked for a long time as well," he mused, and I lolled my head to the side on the arm of the chair, rolling my eyes at him not believing him for a second.

"Oh really? Since when?" I asked, and he ran his fingers through his blond hair, pushing it back.

"That I will drink for," he chuckled as he took a large drink, a grin growing on his face.

"I am drunk. We should stop this, or I will be left with no secrets," I hummed as I closed my eyes, feeling exhausted from the alcohol and lack of sleep.

"The crown prince speaks of you often," he said out of nowhere, and I opened my eyes to watch him stand, striding towards me, the light casting a dark line across half his face. "He plans to proposition you. I will not be involved with you if you accept him," he declared, and I don't know if it was jealousy or something else, but I liked him being so upfront with me, especially while looking so unhinged. But the prince is harmless; he has messed with me for years, so the archduke needn't worry.

"My bedroom is down the hall to the right. If you want to stay, you are more than welcome," I groaned as I stood, not giving him an answer just to mess with him. I walked towards the door, feeling his eyes, and I heard his feet fall in behind me.

"I will not share you," he growled, and I stopped to look at him in shock, his face now fully in the dark, his eyes an icy contrast.

"You act as if this will continue past a few nights. I am still pushing for you to marry the princess, even if she is insane. It is the only way to save my neck," I teased, opening the door, but he moved his hand, pressing it closed.

"It is not the only way," he breathed, now moving into my space, pressing me into the door. His lips were hot on my ear, to lick a trail down to my neck, his hand pulling my ass against his pelvis. I groaned and let him take over my body as the heat from last night swirled in my mind. "Do not sleep with the prince," he whispered along my collarbone before nipping me, and I turned around to look at him.

"Have you imagined doing this before?" I asked, not having expected the words to escape my lips, and he watched me with what looked to be anger again as he undid his belt. The promise of his touch had me reeling.

"That is a cheeky question," he hummed, leaning back to unbutton his shirt; he was now teasing me.

"Are you not going to follow the rules of the game?" I pressed, and he tilted his head slowly, his eyes running the length of my body.

"I can't quite focus on the question at the moment," he mused, sliding his knee between my legs. "Tell me you will not sleep with the prince, and I will answer in kind," he offered and yet I only wished to provoke him more.

"You ask a lot for a man who holds no power over me," I teased. He lifted me and pinned me to the door, his teeth digging into my shoulder as he slid my dress up, exposing my bare ass to his hands. God, he really is a wonderful beast.

"How have you come to think I hold no power over you?" he said harshly against my skin as he pulled my thin nightgown down my chest, so I rubbed my core into his erection to tease him.

"I can show you," I breathed as I ran my hand down his body, pulling his dick free from his pants, and his gaze landed on me as I placed him at my entrance to slide down on him. He groaned loudly as he fully buried himself, and I closed my eyes to adjust to his length. He is so big; it's almost too much.

"I don't know why you think this doesn't give me power over you," he drawled as he slowly moved in me, making me tremble with desire.

"Because you want it just as much as I do," I hummed, and he chuckled against my bare chest before sucking and licking around my nipples.

"I guess you are right," he conceded before taking me to the chaise. He sat, letting me ride him slowly, and I made sure to show him just how much I wanted it as I unbuttoned his shirt, gliding my fingers down his strong chest. I slid off the fabric, and maybe it was the alcohol or being able to see him in the dimly lit room, but he watched me with a look so soft and wanting it was almost scary to witness this powerful man seem so wrapped up in this moment. He was gentle and caressed my skin, kissing and sucking parts of me that I ached to feel a man cherish. "You are beautiful," he moaned, and his face became red as he lulled his head back. "It is impossible not to desire every part of you," he cursed, his face mixed with tortured pleasure. I knew that was a sign he was trying not to cum, but I was so close, and knowing I could give him this satisfaction boosted my ego. "Caroline," he moaned my name, causing butterflies to swirl in me. I could only focus on rocking on him as I gripped his shoulders and ground into him, begging for the friction to give me my release. I cried out into the room, and my orgasm broke, sending shocks of pleasure through my whole being. I crumpled forward onto his sweaty chest, and he gave me a moment before pushing up into me over and over until lifting me to cum on my ass quickly; both of us now satisfied, and yet I could do that again with ease.

He surprised me by letting me back down so I could stay relaxed on his chest as his hand came to play in my hair. "I am exhausted," I murmured before closing my eyes, pretending to fall asleep on him, hoping to make him stay longer. I did not know what else to say or where to go from here because his gentleness was very unsettling. I think I might be able to understand him better if he was less invested in the moment as well because he didn't try to leave.

"I should take you to bed, for I am not done with you, my little spy," he whispered as I felt him pull something over my back. I peeked out from under my eyelashes to see that it was his white dress shirt, and he was bare-chested. He fixed his pants under me, then stood up, holding me in his arms as if I weighed nothing while walking out of my study. "You should be careful with your curiosity," he gritted, and I was about to speak when I heard Janet.

"I mean no offense. I just worry for my madam after how she came home last," Janet spoke nervously, and I had to hide my smile. She was good at this as well; even as she led him to my room, I could hear the way she hesitated her steps in fake fear.

"I see. Well then, I will give you the same warning. Do not tell a soul about what you have seen, or your madam will pay the price," he threatened, and I let out a soft groan to snuggle into his arms, feeling him grip me tighter to his chest.

"Madam values her secrets. I would never go against her. She has been through enough," Janet voiced somberly, and I indeed need to give her a raise for this act...

8

Playthings

He stayed with me until the morning, wrapped around me just like the night before, and of all things, it was comforting. He held me close, his arm anchoring me to him as he breathed me in. It was nice not to sleep alone. The last year had been challenging after losing Ronald, even if I didn't love him...I missed him. However, a void I didn't know I had was being filled right now as Claude's hand caressed my naked body so hungrily it was impossible to be still. What a very strange man to be so soft in the most unexpected ways, especially regarding how much care he gives my body. "I know you are not sleeping," he murmured as he pulled me against his pelvis, taking a deep breath in of my hair. I tried to stay as calm and quiet as possible as he caressed my body greedily. "Caroline, I know you are awake," he breathed into my ear, sending a chill down my spine with the way he said my name. That was the first time he had properly said it besides when he moaned it last night, and I rather liked the sound of it.

"No, I am asleep," I grumbled as I turned in his arms to trail kisses across his muscular chest, and his fingers tightened on my back as if upset.

"I have to leave. Do not get me worked up before my meeting with the crown prince," he warned, which now seemed like a challenge.

"You are *already* worked up," I hummed sleepily before putting my leg over his hip to rub my sex against him. He groaned in desire as he watched me, and then his lips were on mine, kissing me softly. Such a strange man to be so gentle...

I rolled him to his back, straddling him, and he grinned at me before massaging my hips down to my ass. "You know that you make strange noises when you sleep, like a small pig," he teased me, and I was deeply offended by his lie.

"Perhaps I was just so tired from you not leaving me be," I snapped before sinking lower down his body, his eyes never leaving mine.

"Could be," he teased as I took his hard length in my mouth, watching his wanton eyes the whole time. I sucked him long and slow, stroking him with my hand until I waited for him to groan. He surprised me by reaching his hand down to cover my nose, making it impossible to continue to suck, and when I pulled back to breathe, I snorted. "See a little pig," he jested as I was pleasuring him, and I had no idea what to do with that.

"I imagine you don't always make the sexiest of noises," I quipped, shocked when he pulled me up his body so I was sitting back on his lap, his wet dick bounding between us.

"I wasn't lying when I said I had to leave," he groaned, and I shifted to take hold of his throbbing length. "Caroline," he cautioned before I placed him at my entrance, and I sank onto his thick cock. He groaned in pleasure as he pulled my face to his, kissing my lips passionately. "I will be late," he murmured over my lips.

"Then make it quick, your highness," I mocked him as I rode him, feeling the friction quickly give me what I wanted.

"Ugh, you feel so damn good pulsing on me like that. You are so wet, Caroline," he breathed harshly as he gripped my ass, helping me move until he rolled me over onto my back, taking over. He pushed into me deep and slow, stilling at the base as he kissed me passionately, and the moment made me feel hot all over...like I was becoming too emotional. He said he needed to go, yet he was taking his time, making me feel as if he might care for me when he does not.

"Harder," I begged, needing to stop my brain from feeling, and he broke the kiss to smirk down at me.

"I enjoy playing with you," he mused as he grabbed the headboard to slam into me roughly. I cried out in delight, thankful that the emotions slowed, but the pleasure did not, making my neck strain down to my toes. "You like this?" he asked as his blue eyes scrutinized me fiercely, and I nodded yes. He folded my legs over my chest to pound into me so hard his balls hit my ass. "You want to be ravaged?" he questioned as I held my knees to my chest, giving him better access.

"Yes, don't stop," I cried louder, and he groaned in delight.

"Is that why you like to suck my dick so much?" he asked out of the blue, and I could barely focus on anything but the growing pleasure in me.

"No, I like how you control me," I admitted before I thought better.

"Fuck, you are amazing," he cursed loudly before his hand came up between us and squeezed my throat. Choking me how I always desired. "You are just a dirty, little spy," he gritted as his body slammed into me. The second it was hard to breathe, my face became hot, and I began to shake from my extreme orgasm rocking through my body. I gasped under his strong hand, and he only let me breathe when he had to lean back to cum on my stomach. I took a deep breath and curled into a ball of pleasure, never wishing to leave this moment of finally having a man be as rough as I yearned for.

"You are so much better than I ever expected," he praised before rolling me over to clean me off, and I was too exhausted to move.

"You can go to your meetings now," I hummed sleepily as I pulled the sheet over my body, so exhausted I wanted nothing more than to sleep.

"If that is what the lady wishes," he whispered before leaving me alone to nap.

I slept all day after his visit and ate an abundance amount of food before I called the short old man back to my house to give him the names of the three men to follow. But as for Chal, I want him to be killed in a situation for which it would be warranted. With many eyes to witness his fall, I already knew what would ruin him, especially if a male accused him. "Madam, what will you do about the king?" Janet asked as she came into the sunroom with a fresh pot of tea, and I honestly hadn't thought about it. I hope, at some point, the archduke will not mind, and let me say that he likes women, but not that I know with first-hand knowledge.

"I have three weeks, so I might as well tour the garden before cutting the flowers," I declared thoughtfully, and she looked at me in worry.

"I don't think the archduke will kill you...to save your own neck, you should at least tell him what you can," Janet pushed, but I waved her out.

"I know...I know," I muttered as I took a sip of my tea and looked out at the setting sky. The advice was good, and I should listen to it, but I wasn't done letting the archduke play with me. I can't believe I spent two nights with the archduke now. I wonder when I will see him again...

That question was quickly answered later that night when I felt a body slide into my bed. However, the problem was he smelled awful, like smoke and alcohol, not what I wanted to deal with in my exhausted state.

"Ugh, go bathe," I groaned as I pushed him off me, and he grumbled something before going to the bathroom. If he was drinking, this might be a long night if something happened with one of the men.

I rolled over, pulling the chain to call for Janet, who came in a moment later, looking frazzled. "Yes, Madam?" she asked, and I felt bad for waking her because she sounded exhausted.

"What time is it?" I groaned as I sat up, peeking at the flickering light coming from the bathroom.

"Almost three in the morning," she said, stifling a yawn.

"He may kill me with exhaustion. Please send up the leftover bread from dinner and a bottle of wine," I instructed before she shuffled from the room. I pulled on my robe, ambling to the bathroom to see the state of this man who had no business being here so late at night. "To what do I owe the intrusion," I teased, leaning against the door trim to watch him wash up in the tub, dumping water down his body as he stood. I smiled crookedly at him when I noticed he was drunk again and looked to be in a foul mood.

"The prince plans to have you as his partner for tomorrow night's party," he rasped as he looked up at me as if it were my fault.

"I see. Well, he is often disappointed at parties I attend because I very rarely dance with anyone," I chuckled just as my maid came into my room to set down the tray. "Thank you, Janet. Sleep well," I called as she left.

"Will do, Madam," she hummed with a knowing smirk, and I was just glad her room was nowhere close to mine.

"So you will not dance with him?" he asked me, and I shrugged. Sometimes, he asks in front of so many people that I have no choice but to say yes—the archduke knows this is social etiquette.

"Why do you care?" I pressed as I watched him scrub his palms roughly. "It seems silly to worry about. It is not as if I will tell the prince of our arrangement of revenge," I laughed as I walked to grab some wine, hoping to relax whatever foolish notions his words were giving me. I should not be having these feelings for him, and yet I enjoy his jealousy...honestly, I enjoyed him coming to see me at a time like this. "So why are you really here?" I mused after I downed the whole glass, going to fill another to help with my tension.

"Need to drink to stomach seeing me so often?" he scoffed, and I turned to see him standing in the doorway with only a towel wrapped around his waist. I could feel my whole body tense in desire to the point I feared he could hear how hard my heart was beating. This can't be more than a crush, and that is exactly what this feeling is, nothing more than a crush.

"Perhaps," I smiled at him behind the glass. He gazed down at my body longingly before he grinned at me so wickedly that I feared I might not be able to walk tomorrow. I honestly have no idea how I am fine right now after our last row.

"You caused me a lot of issues tonight," he declared, and I didn't dare move, for it felt as if I were caught in a trap that I willingly entered. "In fact, I almost killed the prince over some unwitting provoking," he said deeply as he stepped toward me, and my heart beat faster with the unknown. Was he going to be fast or take his time? "Do you care for your sheets?" he asked, catching me off guard.

What does that even mean?

"I have no particular attachment unless you are trying to kill me. Otherwise, I would like to keep them unspoiled," I laughed, and he frowned at me.

"I am in no mood for that, Caroline," he scoffed as he walked to stand before me, and I was once again reminded how much smaller I was than this massive man. "Go sit on the bed," he ordered, and I bit my lips to hide my excitement from the lust in his deep voice. He must need to relax more than I thought. I did as told, needing to get these feelings of attachment to leave. Hopefully, I will use the beast inside him to save me from my heart's desire to believe everything he says. "Get undressed. This is going to be a long night," he announced, and at that moment, I was lost to my desires.

9

Anticipation

He came to stand in front of me, no longer smelling of a seedy bar but clean like my honeysuckle soap. His blue eyes skimmed down at my naked body in such desire I could see just how much restraint he was using right now. "Would you like to know what he said that bothered me so?" Claude asked, and I wasn't sure I cared, for I could only imagine what the prince could say behind closed doors.

"Not particularly. I do not wish to be as vexed as you," I whispered, and he smirked at me before kneeling on the ground before me.

"You do not care at all?" he asked, and I followed his hands, watching as he pulled the tie from my robe that lay on the floor. "he claims that he can get you to crawl to him, to beg to be filled by him," he mused, and my skin prickled as I held out my wrists for him to tie them which made him smirk so hungrily I was unraveling. "You are such a good girl that I could picture it perfectly, so you can imagine how upsetting it was when my face still smelled of you," he declared, and I nodded slowly.

"I would never crawl to him," I giggled at the idea, and he cocked an eyebrow up as if he didn't believe me.

"We shall see," he scoffed as he stood up. "Open your mouth and close your eyes," he ordered, and I did as told, expecting him to fill my mouth with his hardened length I knew was straining under the towel. My body hummed in anticipation; unexpectedly, I felt a slow stream of liquid run into my mouth. I opened my eyes, shocked to see him pouring the wine on me. I swallowed what was in my mouth, but he continued to pour until it ran down my neck. "See, a good girl who follows orders," he groaned as he stopped to slide one hand between my clenched thighs, "So wet," he cursed, slipping his fingers inside me, and I spread my legs wide for him to do as he pleased because I wanted him to know I desired him.

I closed my eyes, lost to his touch before I felt the wine pour on me again, and I opened my mouth to receive it. His fingers swirled in me deftly, and I undoubtedly enjoyed it when he was jealous. I let the wine overflow my mouth and run down my chest to ruin my bed as he predicted. When his mouth came down to mine, he kissed me deeply, stealing some wine for himself, and it was becoming impossible not to beg him to stop messing with me. "You should see you right now," he groaned, and I opened my eyes to gaze up at him through my lashes. "I want to make you scream my name," he cursed before taking the last swig of the wine, his hand reaching out to grasp my neck roughly, tilting my head up. His other hand pulled from between my legs to open my mouth, his finger shoving down my throat as his other hand choked me. The whole thing was so erotic my body was on fire as I tasted myself mixed with wine. He opened my mouth, allowing me to breathe before he leaned forward to stream the last of the wine from his mouth to mine. "So fucking seductive," he groaned through gritted teeth as I swallowed the wine, wishing for him to fill me after such a display, but he grabbed my hands to untie me. "I think it is better if I go," he grumbled, taking me by surprise as he walked away from me to sit in my armchair by his clothes as if he were still upset after such a build-up.

"Have I done something to offend you?" I asked, and he shook his head as if he were defeated, but I could see plain as day he was turned on. His length was hard and bounding in the air when I wish it were doing that inside me.

I sunk to the floor with the tie still in my hand, unsure of what to do, but I wasn't going to let this end without pleasure. He came here for something, and I plan to get that for myself at least. I crawled on the floor slowly towards him, his eyes watching me intensely. "You are a very good girl," he huffed in irritation, which I did not understand.

"I can be immoral if you like," I whispered as I got closer, and he reached out to grasp my chin.

"It is not that I wanted you to crawl to me. It is that you should crawl to no man," he groaned before pulling me up to his lap. "But now that I have seen it, I fear you may suffer because of me," he whispered over my lips before kissing me deeply, no heat lost between us. In fact, I felt as if I were on fire, my face burning all the way to my toes.

"Tell me what else bothered you," I finally asked as his hand snuck around to cup my ass, his fingers delving back inside me, making me moan with how well he gave to me.

"The more Tristan fantasized aloud, the more I drank," he whispered against my neck as he licked up my ear. "The prince is much more tame than I thought, for he could never satisfy you," he said as his free hand pulled the tie from my clenched hand. I moved my wrists out in front of me, but he shook his head with a smirk. "Behind your back," he said, and I didn't mean to whimper when he pulled his fingers from me to tie my hands, but I was a ball of nerves.

"Claude, I am not such a weak woman," I breathed. He grinned at me, pulling the knot tight, causing me to jump in excitement.

"I would never argue that," he mused as he stood up, taking me to the bed and laying me on my chest. He took hold of the end of the robe, tying it to the footpost of my bed, straining my arms, and for the first time, I was nervous. I never was one not to like being able not to move. I pulled on it to test how tight it was, and he looked at me with an amused smirk. "I will not leave you here forever, so calm down," he affirmed, not easing my worries until I felt him grab my hips, pulling my ass in the air, and his hot mouth began to torment me. "Oh, Caroline, you are soaking wet," he whispered against me, his fingers gripping my hips so I couldn't move, and he was doing as he pleased to me. "He has no idea how sweet you taste," he groaned, and from such a long build-up, I could feel my orgasm…I was so close to cumming.

"He will never know," I moaned, pushing back against his mouth as he pulled my leg into the air so he could suck on my clit.

"I told you I would never share, and I meant it," he cursed, letting me go, my orgasm slowing with his sudden change. "Do not do this with the prince," he groaned as he slammed into me from behind.

"Ah," I whined from the force and pleasure of finally getting what I wanted. "He has nothing I desire," I whimpered as his thighs slapped into me repeatedly, making me move up the bed, my hand straining to hold onto the sash.

"Caroline," he moaned my name, his mouth coming down to bite my back, and I feared I was going to get real feelings for this man other than possession. This is only a crush, I reasoned as he pulled from me, and I was shocked when his mouth went back to my sex. His tongue pushed inside me before sucking on my clit again.

"Oh, god, oh god," I whimpered as my orgasm broke, and I about fell off the bed from losing all control. Claude caught me, untieing my hands to roll me to my back with a smirk on his face that I would never forget. His hand slid down my body until he spread my legs open, all while gazing down at me with lust. His fingers pushed inside me, and I wanted him to be inside me again, not just his fingers. I wanted more as the tension between us did not ease.

"When I pull from you, for a second, your pussy is formed perfectly for my dick," he groaned, his eyes wholly focused before pushing his fingers back inside me, his neck straining as I did my best not to read into his words. His mouth came down to suck on my chest, and I feared I would come again before he was even close. His body covered mine, and that heat again as I put my arms over his shoulders to hug him to me. He moved slowly as if savoring me, and every thrust made me nervous for my heart. "Caroline," he called to me, and I clenched around him when his mouth bit down on my nipple. "Cum for me. I wish to feel you cum around me," he demanded. I had been so close that it wouldn't take much more coaxing. He leaned back to grab my neck, choking me as his other hand rubbed my clit fiercely, still pushing into me slowly. I began to lose air, and my orgasm broke, making me whimper under his hand. "God damn, Caroline," he cursed as I continued to shake. Suddenly, he pulled out to cum on me, and I had never had sex like this before. I was satisfied beyond belief but instantly wanted more...Yet once again, sleep forced me to neglect my desires, well, for a short while anyway.

I awoke in a haze as if I had drank a whole vineyard, and I knew it was more exhaustion than the small amount of wine I was able to imbibe as it was all over the bed or my body. I blinked awake, noting fingers in my hair but feeling the irritating sensation of having to use the restroom. "Claude," I groaned, pushing him back, my mouth dragging against his chest. "I need to go to the bathroom," I managed to say, but I wouldn't really remember much of this moment in the morning as he untangled from me, and I ambled to the bathroom, lost in a haze, too weary to locate the door or summon the will to close it—every fiber of my being throbbed with exhaustion.

I crawled back to bed like some frail creature, landing on Claude's hard body, him in my spot, or truly the spot I needed since I was not going to be moving. "Did you forget I was here?" he mused, and I groaned, holding him to me to feel how sticky we were.

"No," I grumbled, and I was slightly irritated that he wasn't as tired as I was, and it plucked away some of that new pride I had gotten from him. I wasn't built for this constant ravaging. "How are you not asleep?" I muttered, and he rolled me to my back. Even in the soft light of the waning candles, I couldn't bring myself to open my eyes to see what face he was making. Any light was too much at the moment.

"You are naked beside me. It is impossible," he declared, and I chuckled as the very spirit of the word danced through my thoughts.

"Very difficult to deal with or not able to be done," I told the definition, almost feeling bad for him as I sat up on his lap. "So, it is difficult not to touch me?" I mused my hand running down the length of his chest before I shifted onto my knees, grasping his hard cock between us. "thankfully for you, it is able to be done," I whispered as I sank down onto him. In my state, I moved slowly, knowing I looked a mess as I rolled my hips, my fingers clawing into his chest.

I watched as he still looked at me as if I were pure desire, even sticky and covered in wine with wild hair. "Caroline, you are such a good girl," he praised me, and for some reason, that broke me. It stroked something deep, almost primal, that made me wish to give him so much more. I leaned down to cover his body with mine, lifting only my ass to slam into him. I was wild in my movements as I bit his neck, my hands gripping the sheet beside his head for leverage. He moaned deeply, the sound just as feral and guttural, and I could feel he was holding back.

"Claude, don't you want to come to," I moaned, and he took hold of my neck to kiss me deeply, and with so much control, his praise earlier swirling in my head as my body tightened, and I ground down on him. I came hard, my whole body pulsing, and I collapsed onto his chest, unable to think or move. "I can't cum anymore tonight," I whimpered, and he rolled me over to my chest, pressing my face into the mattress before sliding into me once more. I pushed my ass up, arching my back to let him pound me from behind; that was all I could offer him, for I was spent.

"You are going to be sore, Caroline," he warned, and I didn't care in the slightest.

I turned to look back at him with a mischievous smile. "I can take it. I can take anything from you," I moaned, swirling my hips, and he didn't last long after.

He may be a vice—I am not yet willing to quit.

10

Between Two Men

The next day, I slept in late, not waking until afternoon, at which time I got a note from the archduke around lunch saying that John Pultas and Gulter Vandal would be at the same social event this evening that the prince wished I would attend...the event that made Claude so upset. So that was my cue to enter the event to watch and listen for any information on them while riling Claude.

I had dressed in my best beaded gown that hugged every curve and left my hair down in big curls. I looked the temptress, and that's what I aimed for tonight to get what I needed from these men.

I will say that Gulter was easy to get information on. I don't know if embezzlement is enough to let the archduke kill him, but it was a start. After one too many whiskeys, he had mentioned his money would never run out—seeing as his work ebbed and flowed with his majesty's. An ignorant lady might not have known what that meant, but as the wife of the last minister of finance, he just boasted to me that he embezzles from the king.

John, however, was harder to get close to with his wife, always so near and especially wary of me. It didn't help that after the last two days of pleasure, I now wore a grimace from the discomfort of so much physical activity with Claude. I still felt him all over my body, so I looked even more unapproachable when I tried to greet John's wife. "What are you looking at?" a male voice hummed deeply from behind me, and I turned to see the crown prince smiling at me, dressed in a dashing black suit. He had the same blond hair and blue eyes as the archduke, yet they were vastly different. Claude stood a good few inches taller, but their demeanors were remarkably contrasting. The prince was carefree and unencumbered, while Claude was more like a tightly wound beast.

"Mrs. Pultas. She looks very agreeable tonight. I was wondering who made her maternity dress," I lied as I glanced around to see if the archduke was here, now that I knew the crown prince was.

"She looks dull as usual. His mistress dresses better these days," the prince jabbed, and he wasn't wrong that poor Mrs. Pultas has to deal with so much public disgrace. If Claude could kill John for infidelity, this would be a simple case.

The prince looked over me in appreciation, and I didn't shy away, having been used to his open ogling. "But no one is ever as lovely as you," he flirted. Ever since I came of age, he has never hidden his attraction towards me, but he does that with almost all the ladies, so I do not feel special.

"I bet your betrothed would beg to differ," I teased, and he leaned into my space too close for comfort.

"You know it is not uncommon for a man to openly take a mistress after an heir is established," the prince noted, and I turned to look at him, feeling my body throb, but not in want for him.

"Is that a proposition to make me the rival of every woman in this room?" I asked as playfully as possible to avoid offending him since he looked rather serious.

"Or the envy. I sense we would do well. You were always so *spirited.* I am satisfied that you are getting out of the house again," he flirted, and I nodded as I went back to studying the room, hoping the prince would get bored and move on because I would much rather be *another* man's mistress. "Ah, you are here. I didn't expect you," I heard the crown prince say from behind me, and I didn't have to turn to know the deep voice was the archduke.

"Last minute pop-in. My day ended quicker than expected," Claude offered by way of an excuse, but a part of me hoped he was here to see me after what he had said last night, for my body was already tight in anticipation of a touch he might steal.

"Madam La'Blauvelt was just discussing something important with me. Would you mind letting us finish," the crown prince mused, and I turned to look at them both. The archduke examined me with his cold blue eyes, and they looked so very different from when he was moving slowly inside me...when they were filled with hungry lust.

"If you must," Claude remarked before walking away; his eyes never shifted back to me while I was busy looking at his ass in his riding pants. He hadn't changed into a dress suit because he must have come right from work, and the tightness of them was a distracting sight—a sinful sight.

"So, what do you think of my proposal?" the prince continued, and I didn't know how to turn down a prince.

"Your highness, you are unwed and have no heir yet. Perhaps ask again in a few years when it's even imaginable," I said slowly, hoping he didn't see my lack of affection.

"I see. Well, I can't be upset since that is not an outright no," the prince laughed just as Claude came walking back over not a minute later with two glasses of champagne. The prince reached out to take one, but Claude shifted it toward me, and I didn't know if I was allowed to take it.

"It is for the lady," Claude said, shocking us both as we stared at him in disbelief.

"Thank you, archduke, that was very considerate of you," I muttered, feeling nervous from all the eyes on me now that I was between the two most influential men in the empire, excluding the king himself.

"Speaking of drinks, your betrothed was looking for you with a glass in hand," Claude noted, and the prince grimaced.

"Damn," he spat before downing his drink to walk off with a frown.

Claude stayed a mindful distance away from me, but that didn't stop the heat in me from blooming into full-out aching, adding to the soreness I already had. "I think I got Gulter," I whispered, and he nodded once behind his drink, seemingly disinterested. His act was remarkable. We looked like strangers standing beside one another, not two people sharing carnal pleasures in private.

"What did the prince want?" he asked like he didn't care that I just told him I completed one-fourth of the assignment he gave me.

"He wants me to be his mistress, but that is nothing new," I whispered, and I noticed Claude's jaw clench before he downed his drink.

"Remember my warning," he threatened, his tone dark, and I grinned at him sideways before moving away so as not to look suspicious.

"I will as long as I am kept satisfied," I teased as desire now spread all over my body from his gaze.

"That is easy," I heard him murmur as I walked away and almost ran right into the princess.

"You have eyes. Use them," she snarled as she bumped past me, and I sighed in irritation before needing a moment to calm myself after Claude and the crown prince essentially placed a target on me.

I wandered toward the bathroom only to find John Pultas belligerent with his wife out in the open. They were at the end of the hall, and even if he was drunk, the way he behaved toward a pregnant woman was abominable. I moved to lean flat against the wall so they didn't hear me, but how she cried for him to calm down made me feel disgusted to my very soul.

I have gotten numerous letters asking how to enjoy marital obligations, but now that I know how John really is, I imagine one of them was from her. She would be mortified if she knew I saw, and legally, I can not meddle with a husband and wife's arguments, but I hope Claude kills him soon. I need a way to keep her safe because right now, I can do nothing but hope that John will go to his mistress tonight.

I turned around, walking along the wall until I slipped out onto one of the verandas to collect myself after just gaining so much information. What a vile, despicable human. *I wonder what it would be like if every man like him died suddenly. If, with a snap, they were gone, perhaps thrown from bridges and cliffs.*

"What are you thinking about?" I heard Claude's deep voice call from behind me, which made me feel safe after seeing such a thing.

"Killing unscrupulous men," I admitted as I turned to smile at him.

"I see," he chuckled before handing me another drink. "And here I was worried you were taking the crown prince seriously," he noted, and I shook my head in disbelief from his words.

"Don't be so ridiculous. You should not worry about silly things that mean nothing. I am only a baron's widow with barely a title to hold on to. The prince has no actual desire for me besides to try and ruffle the other ladies, so don't worry about things so below your station," I admonished Claude, and his eyes darkened as he glared at me. Why must he always look as if a dark cloud sits atop him?

"You must only pretend to be clever," he mocked me, and I scoffed at his remark.

"Well, I know how to get three of your men now, so you should be thanking me," I announced, hoping for praise, and he shifted closer to me. The tension in me pulsed and snapped the closer he got, and I knew it wasn't wise to stay this close here, but I did.

"Three? You said you only had Gulter," he questioned, and I turned fully toward him to grin, not hiding that I was proud of myself.

"I am a woman of many talents, archduke, very soon you will not need me anymore—" I teased as I went to walk away, "—for we will be finished quickly," I sang, and he seized my hand, hauling me closer to him.

"Have you ever assumed it is not *need*...but *want*," he challenged as his fingers grazed down my arm to draw me closer, but stopped quickly when the prince sauntered out with his fiancé.

"Your highness, Lady Ignis," I bowed in greeting, but Claude made no move to bend since he was on the same social level as them and was already not one to please people with formalities.

"You two seem rather chummy as of late?" the prince questioned with a bite, and a sudden chill ran down my back in fear that being linked to these two wasn't wise. I might be playing with fire when it comes to being between the two men.

"We ran into each other after, so we were continuing our discussion about doing a stop-in for the wounded soldiers," I lied as I took a composed sip of my drink. I really felt like my whole body was humming from almost being caught in Claude's arms.

"And when will that be?" the prince asked as Claude shifted further away from me.

"She was planning for Wednesday around lunch," Claude lied, and I nodded in agreement.

"I look forward to coming to see you enchant so many men with your lovely words," the prince flirted openly in front of his fiancé, and I smiled at him, not knowing what to say.

"Yes, it is fortunate such a woman is so well-versed with her *tongue*," Lady Ignis spat, and I bit my bottom lip to hold back laughter. When I heard Claude's breathy chuckle pulling the crown prince's eyes away from me, I was surprised, and I think we were both equally shocked by the display.

"Jealous ladies can be quite vicious. It almost makes me miss the battlefield," Claude joked, and I let out a chuckle, unable to stop it in the shock of his words.

"I am not jealous of a widowed Baroness who peddles her flesh," Lady Ignis barked, and I flinched at her pointed words.

"I better go find my next victim," I scoffed to save face before walking back into the party and out to my carriage, my body humming with embarrassment. "Thomas. I am ready to go home," I breathed in exhaustion as I rubbed over my neck, excited about the prospects of sleep.

"Right away. Miss, let me just finish watering the horses," he said from where he stood by the large brown horse, and I opened the carriage door to get in. A gold letter sat on the bench, and my stomach dropped at the sight of it.

Two Weeks

F

That was all it said, and my hand began to tremble from the warning. The king wanted an answer, but I didn't know if I could give it.

11

To Love a Rose

The next morning, when I awoke, Claude was sitting in a chair opposite my bed with a tumbler of alcohol so early in the morning that I feared something awful may have happened. He startled me with his dark presence, and when I sat up, pulling the blankets around my naked body, he glared at me. "Tell me about Lord Gulter," he commanded, and I was surprised to see him in the same clothes as last night, looking so upset. When did he get here?

"He is embezzling from the king to cover his gambling debts," I said, and he nodded as if he believed me before holding his tumbler to his forehead; it was plain to see that he was irritated.

"Then I will have cause," he murmured, and I agreed, but if the archduke goes and kills these four men, it will draw a lot of attention to him, even if the deaths are justifiable. It could cause a war between our country and Claude's homeland.

"I have an idea about it," I said as I leaned over to grab my hair clip and secure it before pulling on my glasses.

"I am all ears," Claude grumbled, and he didn't sound happy in the least as I brought a pen and paper from my side table with me.

"Pay off Lord Gulter's loan sharks for the debts he has left. Then they will kill him, so you are not directly involved," I stated, and his lips quirked up into a smile as I wrote down what I knew of the men to send him home with. He stood up and walked toward me, and I was so distracted by his size I forgot to speak.

"You are very cunning," he complimented, setting down his empty drink to pull off his tie before tugging his white button-down shirt over his head.

"I just read often," I said, and he shook his head no as he crawled up the bed toward me.

"No, you are very clever," he breathed over my lips before pulling me up to his lap to claim my mouth. When my blanket fell away, revealing my unclothed body to his hands, he groaned into the kiss. "If I had known you were naked, I would have done this hours ago," his words sent a jolt through my stomach as they were muffled by the hungry kiss.

So, he was here for a long time. God, I should not like that so much. "I usually sleep nude," I rasped as he began to kiss down my neck, pulling me onto his lap, where he knelt before me. I wrapped my legs around his waist, sliding down onto him so we became one.

"Caroline," he whispered between kisses, sucking down my neck, and the way he moaned my name was indescribably sexy. His hands tightened on my back as we rocked together, and he held me against him fiercely. This moment felt a lot like the last time he worshiped my body, making me uncomfortable in my feelings of pleasure from his caress. "I wanted to dance with you," he breathed as he licked a line down my neck to my nipple before sucking it into his mouth, making me cry out with his arms hugging me tightly to his body. "I want to touch you in front of others," he said, and I threw my head back, pushing my breasts into his face. I was surprised when he reached up to unclip my hair, and the moment seemed slowed as our sweaty bodies held each other. My hair fell around us, and he fisted it as he pushed up into me harder. "Caroline," he groaned again, and his calling to me drove me crazy.

"Claude," I cried, grinding down on him harder as my orgasm grew, and it began to slowly break. I bucked against him franticly to hold onto the feeling as I bit his neck so as not to scream.

"You are driving me crazy wearing your glasses," he cursed just as the door opened to Janet's shocked face, and he stilled so deep inside me I felt him throbbing. "Shit," he cursed, his body slamming up into mine as his head landed on my shoulder.

"Oh, s-sorry, Madam," Janet exclaimed before rushing out the door, closing it behind her. I was shocked by Janet's intrusion, so the euphoria of my orgasm was pushed aside; instantly nervous that he was upset we were caught in the act.

"Well, that was a first," he grumbled, and I turned to look up over the side of his relaxed face.

"She will knock next time," I affirmed as he moved my hair to the side to kiss softly down my neck.

"No, I came inside you," he drawled, and I didn't know what to say to that, but Ronald had all the time. Never once did I become pregnant.

"Well, it matters not," I chuckled as he moved us to lie in bed, and there was a very strange look in his eyes.

"Are you not worried?" he asked, and I shrugged.

"I didn't lie when I said my husband and I tried our hardest for a child," I whispered, and he nodded before tucking my head under his chin to play with my hair.

"I see," he whispered before hugging me tighter to his muscular chest.

I don't know what he was thinking after what we just did because of all things; this man's gentleness towards me is so illogical. If I could describe it to someone, I would say that it felt like making love, but we don't know each other well enough for that. This closeness was so very scary, and after the letter from the king, I was having a hard time not feeling a pit of fear grow in me. "What is your schedule for the rest of the week?" he asked as his lips brushed over my forehead.

"Today, I plan to see Lady Pultas and confirm my hunch. Then, on Wednesday, I will meet the wounded men, and the rest of the week will remain open to opportunity." I hummed, and he nodded before I heard his breathing even out. I think he must have fallen asleep.

I lay there trapped in his arms for a long while until I was able to pry my body out and move to grab my robe. I looked back at his large body, sleeping soundly in my bed before I opened my door to walk down to breakfast. "Janet," I called as I strode in to find my tea cold after having been so late to eat.

"Madam, I am so sorry. If I had known, I wouldn't have come in," she said nervously. I nodded in understanding. She would never be so intrusive.

"I know. Please warm my tea and have something prepared for when he awakens," I ordered, and she scurried off, leaving me alone. Why was he here and not at his home again? And why did he look so upset? Whatever the issue, he seems exhausted, so I should let him sleep. *Sleep helps everything.*

When Janet walked back in with a steaming cup of tea, I smiled at it in excitement. "Will you draw me a bath after work and send a letter to Lady Pultas asking if she will come for lunch," I requested, and Janet nodded yes before smiling at me.

"Will do, Madam," she said, and as much as I missed managing a large estate, having Janet, Garth, the cook, and Thomas, my driver, was more than enough for just me.

I ate in comfortable silence, reading over my letters—getting ahead of work for the day, which made me feel slightly accomplished after the last few days of lounging.

After two hours, I was shocked when Claude walked into the dining room without a shirt on. "You left me again," he murmured before he came to kiss my cheek and sit beside me. The ease of the moment twisted in me, and I was dumbfounded by how comfortable he was with being so affectionate. How is he so okay with this? Why is he doing this? And I came to the conclusion that this man must be crazy...

"I didn't want to wake you," I whispered as this moment reminded me of a time when I used to never eat alone.

"I came to sleep beside you, not alone in your bed," he grumbled before taking the paper I had already read.

"I see, and when did you get here?" I asked just as she walked in with a plate of food for him. Janet couldn't make eye contact as she set down the food and scurried out in fear, which bothered me. "I wish she wasn't so frightened of you," I sighed, and he looked up at the door where she had run out.

"Does it bother you so?" he asked, and I nodded before opening the next letter. "She will get used to me," he stated as if this were going to be a common occurrence.

"You are very bold," I teased before turning back to the letter to read while fighting the urge to read into his words.

~Madam

I have found myself in love with a woman who is much too beautiful and adored by all. Everywhere I take her, she is showered with affection. ~

She says I am being ridiculous for being so jealous. What can I do to help her see my mind? ~

I chuckled at the letter, drawing Claude's attention as he took a large bite of his steak. "What is so amusing?" he asked as I dipped my pen in my ink.

"This poor man, he is going to suffer as long as he loves this woman," I mused. "He says he loves the town beauty, and she gets much too much attention. To me, he just sounds jealous," I giggled, and Claude looked at me with a smirk.

"I can empathize. You yourself draw an irritating amount of attention," he joked as I placed my pen on the paper for too long, making an ink dot—for his words shocked me. At this moment, I didn't know what to say back to Claude, so I wrote.

~ To love a rose is a noble cause indeed. Remember that even the most beautiful things can wilt if given too much attention.

Try not to put too much stock in what others think of the one you love because looks will fade, but your love should not. Try to curb your jealousy, or it could lead to resentment.

Madam La'Blauvelt~

I finished the letter, and Claude held out his hand like he wanted to read it, which made me feel uncomfortable for some reason. But I reluctantly handed it over, feeling anxious as he read it with no expression. "Better said than done. You must not really understand how truly devious men can be to steal *a rose,* as you say," he mused before handing it back to me.

"Then what would you tell the man?" I asked, feeling irritated by his critique.

"I would say the same, but do something much more shocking," he declared as he went back to eating.

"Which is?" I asked, and he grinned at me darkly.

"Men cannot compliment without a tongue nor see without eyes. Any unwanted advances should be nipped in the *bud* quickly," he teased with a serious tone, and I gulped hard at his idea. "So do not indulge the prince, or things could become more messy than necessary," he warned me, and I stared at him in confusion.

"Are you saying you are jealous of how the prince looks at me?" I asked, and his grin did not leave his handsome face.

"I am," he admitted, and I didn't know what to feel as my body tingled from his words. "And I got here at four," he continued as he set down his fork. I must have been staring at him strangely because his grin persisted as he stood up to walk toward me. "I don't know what you thought this was, but I plan to keep you," he mused as he leaned over me in the chair, his breath tickling my lips.

"Oh," was all I could manage before he kissed me fervently, his hand coming to tighten on my neck. Suddenly, a knock sounded at the door, and he groaned before letting go.

"Madam, your bath is ready, and Lady Pultas agreed to your lunch date. I'll head to the market to get the food she prefers in her pregnant state," Janet announced through the door.

"Thank you. Be safe, and take Thomas with you," I ordered, and she agreed before leaving us alone.

"Your staff is much more useful than mine," he whispered before stretching, drawing my attention to his long body.

"Are you really 6'5?" I asked without thinking, and he turned to laugh at me.

"You are a truly amusing lady. Go take your bath before I fuck you on this table," he teased me, and I stood up, dropping the robe, making his eyes flash in want.

"How disappointing," I laughed as I walked out of the room toward the bathing chambers and heard him follow.

When I got in the tub, I left the door open so I could watch Claude dressing in a completely different suit. "Did you bring other clothes?" I called out to him.

"Yes, I like to be prepared," he said before turning to look at me with lust in his gaze.

"And you just knew I would let you stay?" I questioned as I lifted my leg to rub down it as a show for him.

"I had a feeling," he murmured before walking into the small room and gently grabbing my foot, rubbing over the sole.

"Lord Claude..." I began, and he leaned down, kissing my ankle.

"Just Claude, Caroline," he drawled before letting my leg go back into the water.

"The king has sent a threat to me. I hope you understand that this secret I keep for you could kill me," I admitted, and his back straightened as a look of anger flashed behind his blue eyes.

"It won't come to that," he declared before leaving the bathing room. "I hope to come for dinner," he mentioned as he pulled on his jacket roughly.

"I'll set a plate for you," I called just as he closed the door behind him and went off to work. Yes, a very, very strange man...

12

A Warning to Take Seriously

Lady Pultas arrived right at lunchtime with a fresh bruise on her wrist that I could see she tried to hide with ruffled sleeves. She made small talk but was wary of me as this was our first time having a private meeting. However, the niceties only last for so long. "I would like to explain why I invited you here," I began as I pushed a small box toward her on the table. "Your husband has been going around saying he is going to have you killed before that baby is born," I lied, but she didn't seem shocked by what I said. She merely let tears slip down her face as she clutched her belly. "In that box is a key to my brother's country estate; it is small and not well kept, but you are free to use it temporarily until you can escape," as she reached to grab it, I put my hand out to stop her. "But why should he be the one to win? Gloria, you have another option," I advised. Her hands began to tremble in mine, and I needed to play this perfectly, or she could tell her husband, and all this would get me killed. "There is a place on Cowlds Street. A small brownstone with pink shutters, this is the house your husband frequents. Where he keeps his mistress, perhaps if something were to happen to them instead, you could keep your life and save your baby," I whispered. She looked beaten, much too docile to be able to carry out a hit on someone, and yet the fear in her eyes gave me hope she would at least keep this discussion between us. "From one woman to another. The key is yours, but I wouldn't run. Your child will be safer and protected by his wealth, so do what you can to save you both. You come from an affluent family. Ask for help," I implored before letting her take the box with the key into her hands.

"You saw then? What he was doing last night?" she questioned, her hands trembling as she stared at the box.

"A man like him is no man at all. What I saw will not be repeated beyond this room," I vowed, and she nodded once before standing. "He said three days. He said he would kill you with his bare hands in three days if he had to. He was very drunk, but he gave details. Please stay safe," I lied again, and this time her hands shook wildly. "Don't let him win," I whispered, and she looked around nervously before stepping closer to me to take my hand.

"I know what I must do. I have thought of it often. Thank you for your counsel. You are better than everyone says," she whispered before she bowed, leaving the room without another word. Let's hope she handles that one for me, one less monster in the world.

Dinner was ready at six, which we held later for him, but Claude wasn't here yet, and I wasn't used to waiting on a man to eat, so I didn't. "Janet, can you cover this and take it to the kitchen to stay warm," I requested just as Claude came walking through the door with a scowl.

"Sorry, I am late. The prince would not leave me be," he grumbled just as he came into the room, tugging off his tie and rolling his sleeves up, his jacket already off. The show of it was so very seductive that even Janet watched in fascination as he came closer to kiss my cheek; the gentleness of the kiss flustered me as he sat down to his plate.

"I will take it to reheat, my lord," Janet offered, but he shook his head no.

"I am the one who is late. This is fine," he said kindly to her, and it was shocking to see him so happy after just looking upset. How can he be okay eating cold food? Is this something from the military? He is much less finicky than any other nobleman I had met. Ronald would only drink his tea at a specific temperature and sent it back often, which I knew used to irritate Janet. "So, how was your lunch with Mrs. Pultas?" he asked before taking a bite of his now cold chicken.

"I am hopeful she will make the right choice," I said as I sipped my wine, and his eyes followed my glass.

"Which is?" he asked as he forked a carrot that was also no doubt cold.

"A secret," I teased, and he grinned at me before taking another bite of his food. "Will you be staying the night again?" I asked, and he watched me for a moment.

"I had hoped," he admitted, and I smiled at him.

"Janet, have water sent to the bath," I called out to the kitchen.

"Will do, madam," she yelled back as he returned to eating, and I poured him a glass of wine before pushing it toward him.

"How was your day besides the prince being a nuisance?" I asked, and he grinned at me wider.

"Lord Gulter shot himself at lunch. I merely gave him a small bit of proof he had embezzled that I was able to uncover in the few hours after I had gotten to work. So that is one down. Congratulations on your victory, little spy," he commended, and I did feel bad for Lord Gulter, but then again, he was much too stupid to have taken over after Ronald. To steal from the king was punishable by death.

"This is yours as well, my lord," I smiled as I drank my wine quickly and stood up to walk toward him, wanting to test his reaction. He scooted back in his chair, and I was shocked when he pulled me to his lap, his hand caressing the back of my neck. "You are very domestic for a man who has never been tied to a woman," I hummed over his lips.

"I am just enjoying you taking care of me. Anyone would want that," he mused before kissing me, his large hand controlling me while his tongue pushed into my mouth, swirling and making me ache for him even after this morning. "Do not come in this room," Claude called through the door, and

I hoped Janet heard him because when he lay me on the table to spread me out to eat, I was not about to have him stop. "You know I have thought about this most of the day. I was not very productive," he whispered as he licked and sucked up my thigh to the apex of my legs. "Your pussy is so delicious I could scarcely get through a meeting without the memory of your moans clouding my sanity." he cursed as his hand slowly pushed my dress up, and the look in his eyes was pure desire.

"Too bad you were so late then," I teased as he kissed my clit, sucking me softly, swirling his tongue in a way that made me want to beg him. His finger slid and curled inside me, and I whimpered from the feeling of him pleasuring me so deftly.

"I will make sure to be prompt the next time," he kissed my lips as he circled his tongue and began to suck. He did that as if to tease me, building me up before doing slow circles to tease me.

"Claude. I love how you play with me," I moaned, and he slowed again, running his hands all over my body under the dress.

"And?" he asked before sucking on me again to the point I couldn't control my legs from sticking straight out, so close to a release.

"I-I. Oh, Claude, you are driving me crazy let me cum," I begged him, and he groaned against my clit before standing up and pushing into me. His arm curled around my lower back, hugging me to him as he fucked me slowly; the friction of our touching made me want more.

"You are so lovely when you beg me," he mused as he began to pull open the buttons on the front of my dress to trail kisses across my chest. Slow torment, he was tormenting me.

"Claude, I can't take it. I give in, please," I cried, and he bit my chest before his hand came up to my neck. His hand tightened, taking away my air as he pushed into me with long and deep strokes. My legs tightened straight out again, and my toes cracked as my whole body felt like it was a string pulled too taut.

I reached between us to quickly rub on my clit, and he leaned back to watch me in his own desire, with his hand still choking me. "Look at you being such a good girl," his hand tightened as he pushed into me. "Cum for me," he commanded, and then I felt it break. My back bowed off the table until he pulled me up to slam harder, his face tucked into my neck as he cradled my head. My body gave out on me, and all I could do was lay relaxed in his arms as he used me. I was fully sated and wanted him to get to feel this release as well. "Caroline," he moaned my name as he came, his teeth sinking into my shoulder, and I burned for this man.

After his bath, he had come out in just his briefs to where I was lying on the bed reading a book. "You are very sweet-looking wearing your glasses," he complimented before lying in bed beside me.

"It is fortunate to look so sweet, then no one knows how dirty I can be for you, my archduke," I mocked, making him grin before he lay back in the bed.

"The prince has said you will accept his offer after he sires an heir," he said out of the blue, and I nodded slowly, having to reread the last sentence I was on.

"I said I would think about it after he sires an heir. I am not in any position to tell a royal family member no," I reminded him before closing my book and turning to blow out my candle.

"Did you not heed my warning at all?" he grumbled, and I rolled my eyes before feeling his arm pull me closer to him.

"I am sure the prince will get over me by then," I said as I tucked against his arm, and this moment felt surprisingly calming.

"He has watched you and flirted with you since you came of age and even after you were married," Claude scoffed as if he knew that for a fact.

"How is it you think you know so much about me?" I asked, and his fingers stroked long lines down my naked back, only making me love this closeness more.

"The prince is quite loud," he grumbled before stilling his hand on my lower body, and at some point, I fell asleep in his arms...

13

The Widow's Lover

He had stayed at his own house the next night, and I didn't see him again until I had come to meet all the wounded soldiers. I had figured it was a noble cause, and very soon, if the king started trying to vilify me, at least I could have my charity to help save what would be left of my reputation. That is unless I just tell the king...or he kills me...or Claude...I shuddered at the thought, throwing myself into each wounded soldier's stories. Some were harder to stomach than others, but behind them all, I saw my brother Paul. So, talking to them was therapeutic, as if they were my family. They were kind to me, making it easy to talk to them, and I was happy to bring some levity to their day.

The large room had at least 20 beds, all filled with soldiers, and thankfully, with so many windows, the room didn't feel like a hospital. If anything, it reminded me of an old school house. However, it was a shock to see so many wounded, but then again, they did make it back from the battle, and that is what all families wish for.

I will say the amount of blood on the wounds they had was hard not to shy away from, and after the last man, I had to go wash up at the back sink, giving me a moment to compose myself. "I heard that you came earlier than expected," the crown prince's mischievous voice mused from behind me just as I was washing the blood from my wrist.

"Yes, I wanted to make sure I had a good amount of time," I whispered just as I saw Claude walk in at the other side of the room. Jeez, it is like they can sense each other. "Excuse me for a moment. I was just going to the last row. It was lovely to see you," I said sweetly as I breezed past him while ignoring Claude with his scowl. Shouldn't they be working in the main building? This is far enough away; judging by their riding clothes, they must have ridden here. I do not understand them, especially when the crown prince is probably only here to mess with me, and Claude is making it worse by being here to witness. It will only make the prince bother me more for the show of it.

The last four men I talked with were very gracious, but what made me uncomfortable was the crown prince and Claude glaring at each other and me the whole time. By the end, I just wanted to go home and nap because of how exhausting they were being.

When I went to leave, I opted for the door behind me so I didn't have to see the two royal men, who thankfully had begun talking to each other as they waited. However, I used it as an escape, walking down the long stone corridor to get to Thomas, whom I hoped would be prepared to depart quickly. "Madam La'Blauvelt," the crown prince called just as I had opened the back door, and I watched as his smile grew the closer he got to me. Claude emerged from the same door a moment later to lean in the opening, watching us.

"Crown prince," I bowed, and he tilted his head as if slighted by my leaving.

"You did not say goodbye," he said woefully as he reached for my hand, and I allowed him to take it to kiss.

"You both were so engaged. I did not wish to interrupt," I said with a fake smile before taking my hand back.

"We were just speaking about the latest gossip. Did you hear that John Pultas's townhouse was burned down last night? He and his mistress didn't make it," he informed me, and I didn't have to pretend to be shocked because I truly was. I never thought Mrs. Pultas could have done something like that, but when I looked up, I saw Claude shift and knew he had helped her somehow. That is why he was gone last night...well, maybe not. He wouldn't stay with me every night; it could have been Mrs. Pultas. She seemed uncompromising in saving her baby.

I could barely form words as I held my breath, feeling unnerved that somehow this might come back to me, even if it was just guidance I had offered. "Oh, that is terrible. I don't know what to say," I whispered before taking my fan out to cool myself. A rush of unease heated my sanity, and it didn't help that Claude came over to us. His presence dominated my already frayed senses.

"Don't be so uneasy. Everyone knows he had it coming," Claude declared, and I blanched at his words just as he reached out, stilling my wrist with the fan to examine my chest. "I am more curious as to what this is?" Claude touched my collarbone, drawing the prince's eyes to follow the contact.

"Do not touch her so freely," the crown prince snapped, thankfully pulling Claude's hand back from me, or I might scorch under his touch.

"I just was wondering if she had blood from the men on her, yet it appears to be some type of love bite," Claude poked, and I had no idea why he was doing this. Why would he provoke the prince like that? I took a hesitant step back and kept my fan to my chest, feeling the need to create space. "Perhaps all your affections are wasted, my lord, if she is previously entangled with another male," Claude dug in deeper, and I was too shocked to object due to his reckless words.

"I am late for a meeting. I really best be going," I murmured, disregarding both men, who began to make jabs at one another regarding my affections, and I could not stand to listen.

I slammed the door behind me, storming off to Thomas, wanting nothing more than to go home as quickly as possible. Who does he think he is to put me in a position like that? Does he find it amusing to frighten me and provoke the prince? I can't even be pleased about the victory with Lord Pultas because of how infuriated I am right now! I need to get out of here quickly; just sitting here makes me nervous.

"Madam," I heard Claude's voice just as Thomas had gotten the horses ready to head out.

"Shit," I cursed under my breath as I straightened in the seat to watch Claude stride closer to my carriage.

"Caroline," he crooned wickedly as he pulled open my door to lean in.

"What is wrong with you? How could..." His forceful kiss left me speechless; his tongue swirling in my mouth as his hand forcefully held my face.

"I'll be there for dinner," he said before pulling back from the embrace, closing the door without further explanation. He left me completely confused, very upset, and slightly turned on...

14

Punished

Despite how turned on I was, I knew that I couldn't let him win like that. So when I got home, I changed into a nice dress and told the staff to expect Claude, but I decided to have dinner by myself. I knew he would be getting there soon, expecting me to be docile and delighted to see him, but that wasn't me. Especially not after what he did! So I took the book I wanted to finish and ate until I was stuffed and drank until I was drunk at my favorite cafe. I stayed at my table reading well into when I usually sleep. Ultimately, I knew I was being petty and needed to return home, but he really upset me.

Thankfully, Thomas, always the gentleman, escorted me to the front door before settling the horses, and I ambled to my room, wondering if Claude had stayed. My thoughts were answered when I saw him sitting in bed reading over a stack of papers. "Look who came home," he said with an astonishingly wide grin; I figured he would be displeased, but he didn't seem to be.

"You are a very peculiar man," I murmured as I went to undress, feeling uneasy on my feet, incapable of getting my dress off without Janet.

"Are you drunk, Caroline?" he asked as he stacked his papers on the bedside table before getting up. Moreover, I was still fighting my zippers, and it only made him grin at me wider, which was aggravating.

"I am a bit. I can do what I please," I remarked with a deep sigh when he came over and unzipped me effortlessly; just a slight touch from him had me aching for more.

"Whoever said you couldn't?" he asked with a grin that was much too sexy.

"You have some nerve, you know. With your face and your chest, and...and I can't think when I look at you. Take off your clothes," I demanded, feeling irrationally turned on by him. I watched as a smug grin plastered his face, and I was slowly becoming senseless.

"Did you miss me?" he teased as he took off his pants, and I shimmied out of my slip so I was naked.

"I simply want you to make me cum," I breathed out as he reached to take hold of my neck, his fingers tightening; until I groaned, his control was intoxicating.

"*Simply*?" he chuckled before pulling me roughly against his chest. "Nothing is simple about making sure you are pleasured before me," he whispered over my lips before kissing across my cheek, and it became hard to breathe under his grasp. "I have to use all of my control to not act on my needs," he said before pushing me down to the bed, so I was on my side. "And when you try to rile me, it makes me only wish to fuck your face leaving you *needing* me," he groaned as he crawled up the bed, grabbed my head shoving his dick into my mouth. With how hard he held my head, I enjoyed every second, even wishing he did it harder. "I wanted to give you a gift tonight for being such a good girl, but after you left me like this, I am not so sure," he rasped as he spanked my ass, making me cry out on his dick. Claude was so gentle the last few times, yet now he was dominating—he really must have waited up for me if he was so pent up. "I think you like to be selfish," he spat as he reached over, spanking me. "even though you look like an angel," he grinned as he spanked me again.

"Ah," I whimpered, only allowing him to shove his dick deeper into my throat.

"Open wider so I can fuck your face," he cursed as he grabbed my hair, making my eyes water in the best of ways before his legs began to tighten, and I figured he was getting close. "There you go, my dirty little spy," he murmured as it became impossible to breathe, and he pushed in all the way to the base so my nose touched his skin, making me gag. "was that worth pissing me off all day?" he questioned darkly as he leaned back pulling my mouth off him with a pop. He rolled me over by my hair so I was flat on my chest. He pushed into me roughly, making me cry out, "I am going to make you cum so hard you miss me more often," he declared as he bit my back, and he knew just what he was doing. He was driving me crazy to make me admit I was being a brat. So I pushed back, matching his fierceness, needing him to know I love this, and he surprised me by pulling out and dragging me on top of him backward. "God damn it, Caroline," he groaned as I sank onto him, and his hand spread me apart roughly. "Your ass is..." he cursed as I moved down onto him, quickly throwing my hair back, and he took hold of the strands as he slammed up into me. He leaned up as his fingers came to hook in my mouth, pushing down my throat as he gently kissed my cheek, the two mixes of emotions driving me crazy as tears of pleasure wetted my face. "I don't think you will ever behave," he growled as he threw me forward onto my hands and knees and began to slam into me harder, his hand wrapping around to choke me. "But I like when you are bad," he breathed against my back. "You deserve to be punished, don't you, Caroline?" he rasped.

"Claude. I am good. I'll be good for you," I whined as I pushed back harder, wanting to cum after being so on edge.

"Fuck," he swore as his teeth came to bite my back, and I lost control. I shook wildly, my legs unable to move, making me fall flat on the bed, but he didn't stop moving, making my orgasm continue to come even after he let go of my throat. "You can do it. Keep moving, baby," he coached me through, making my orgasm continue, "Hold tight and focus on every pulse of me deep inside you," he commanded, and I focused on that sensation, not wanting to let it go. "Caroline," he moaned my name as he came, his teeth sinking into my shoulder as his weight pressed me into the bed. I closed my eyes to catch my breath, and he didn't move for a while until he began to kiss my neck gently up to my sweaty face. "My lovely little spy," he whispered against my lips, making me never wish to give this up. I have no idea what is going on with us or how this is going to continue, but what I do know is that I really enjoy how he makes me cum...

The following morning, when I awoke, I felt worse for wear, barely able to roll out of bed, and if I were to vomit, it would be a welcome relief. "Janet. I think I am dying," I groaned as the headache came.

"Yes, Madam?" she called after a moment, entering the room with a tight-lipped grin. "Did you have fun last night?" she admonished me as she handed me a glass to drink.

"I don't need to hear it from you," I grumbled before taking the cup and drinking it fiercely, only for it to burn horrendously. "Ugh, what is this?" I spat as I looked at the cloudy water in vexation.

"The archduke said it would help," she said with an even bigger grin, and I rolled my eyes, holding my nose to swallow it.

"And what is this nasty thing?" I asked as I handed the empty glass back.

"Rice water, ginger, and apple vinegar," Janet stated before I fell back into the bed, my stomach feeling hot.

"What a horrid man," I grumbled before pulling the blanket back over me.

"I think he is surprisingly agreeable," Janet murmured before leaving, and I hated that I agreed with her.

I didn't get out of bed until after lunch, and I was thankful Garth only gave me bread to eat but also that nasty drink again. I hated to admit that it was helpful. It had been a long time since I got so drunk, and being hungover is for the young, which I am not.

When I rolled over to the side of the bed, I saw a note that I hadn't noticed before, and when I looked it over, I knew it was from the archduke.

~Last night was fun, but I think I need to give you a break. I'll see you at the gala Friday, Little Spy~

That is tomorrow night, and I am not looking forward to seeing the crown prince or dealing with anything that involves the royal family. The king will want answers.

By the next day, I felt back to normal even though I slept poorly, secretly hoping the archduke would show up to eat dinner or stay the night. It was dangerous how much I liked having him around. I couldn't stop thinking about him, which was exceedingly vexing. Like when I poured a cup of coffee, mixing in the cream, it frothed a bit, and I smiled at the dirty thought of me sucking Claude off until he climaxed. But I stopped when Janet rushed to the room, looking startled. "Are you okay?" I asked as I went to stand up, but the crown prince strolled in right after her with a large smile. I closed my silk robe, which I wore in case

Claude showed up, and the prince bowed slightly to me, his eye tracking the movement. "Janet, please make some tea and bring out some snacks," I ordered. She nodded yes as she ran away, and I felt wildly underdressed, especially after Claude's warning.

"A timid one she is," the crown prince laughed before his eyes swept over me. "Sorry to intrude, but I felt this was best to bring up here and not tonight at the event," he said as he sat without my offering.

"What can I do for you?" I asked, feeling uneasy because the last time he came to visit was when I was still married, and he had made a rather inappropriate proposal back then to give me a child.

"It is what I can do for you," he said arrogantly as he leaned back, looking around my small dining room as if judging me. My unease grew as to how he learned where I lived now. "I heard from Count La'Blauvelt himself that you were given nothing besides your dowry after your husband's passing," he began, and I gulped hard because I had hoped to have another year before people began to find out. Even if the archduke knew, it had made sense because he was trying to find a way to kill the count, but the prince should not be delving into my personal affairs like this.

"I am doing well and enjoy the freedom I have. So I am embarrassed that you worried for nothing, your highness," I said as sweetly as I could before Janet walked in, looking just as unsettled as before.

"I see," he said, obviously not expecting my answer. He leaned back and looked me over again as if trying to figure something out, and under his stare, I felt especially uneasy. "If you have a lover, that can be taken care of," he threatened, and my hand trembled under the table, not out of fear for Claude because the prince would never kill the archduke, but because the crown prince could kill one of my staff thinking it was them. What if he kills Thomas, assuming it is him...or Garth, my cook? He is still young. They have done nothing wrong, and a simple accusation could ruin their lives.

"Have you spoken to the king about the assignment he has given me?" I asked as I tried to hide my fear, but I could only try to protect those I cared for with what I had.

"My father?" he questioned as he leaned forward in curiosity.

"Yes...I would consult him before continuing your pursuits of me," I cautioned as I leaned to pour him a cup of tea.

"I see..." he gritted as he scrutinized my neck, which still had signs of Claude's mouth on me. "Then we will talk more at the event tonight. Save me a dance," he snapped as he got up, leaving just as fast as he came.

Once I heard the door slam, I slumped forward onto the table. "Madam, are you okay? Should I send a letter to the archduke?" Janet asked as she came to rub my shaking shoulders. What she didn't understand was that even if Claude liked to enjoy my body and didn't hate me, he would never help me if he knew I had to betray him. This was doomed from the start because, in all reality, he was a paid job which made me a whore, and yet I pretended like this meant more to us both because I became his spy.

"No, no one can save me from what I must do," I stated as I pushed up from the table. I will have to make a statement, and I will need to look the part because I am playing with fire, so it will only get worse before it gets better. Let's just hope they don't kill me, I thought as I rubbed my neck.

15

The Wrath of a King

I was dressed in a black velvet dress that hung off my shoulders, hiding none of the marks Claude left on me, and at this point, my only way to live was to force everyone's hand to the light. That was the only plan I could think of all day, and it was hard to think under duress. If I am lucky, they will all take pity on me, but I am not holding my breath. This very well could be my last day as a madam or even alive. My stomach ached and rolled as if I already knew the outcome, but I had to hold on to hope that they would just find all this amusing so as not to kill me or maim me. "Madam, I don't know why you don't just ask the archduke for help?" Janet cried as she sat beside me in the carriage, and I hated the rocking. It only made me feel more queasy in this troubling time.

"The archduke has no loyalty to me and definitely won't after tonight," I muttered as the carriage stopped, and I took one last deep breath before Thomas opened the door to help me out. "Just be safe," I whispered to Janet, who looked ready to cry.

"NO, you be safe," she implored, and I closed the door, unable to listen to her sobs without doing the same. But I held my head high as I pulled the hem of my dress up and walked into the large dance hall of the king's castle. The stares of many seared into me, yet I made no attempt to shy away from their open gawking.

"What are you doing? Why are you wearing that," Claude snarled when he came up behind me, and I flinched under his sore tone.

"I am saving my neck," I retorted as I walked away, feeling his hand reach for me, but I shifted quicker. I didn't even make it a minute into the party before he was behind me, pursuing me to the drink table.

"Caroline, what are you doing?" he questioned darkly as I grabbed a glass of wine, and his blue eyes were full of irritation as he tried to fight with me.

"Are you sending the prince to mess with me and only pretending to care that he is interested in me? Because you said it wouldn't get to this point, and yet here we are," I scoffed, and his eyes widened from my accusation as if he understood what was about to happen.

The princess quickly stepped beside Claude, having followed us, but he paid her no mind as his hot stare reminded me of the last time we slept together—a beast.

"Archduke Sidmund, I was waiting for you on the other side of the room, and I was hoping you would indulge me in a turn around the floor," Princess Flora asked at the worst possible moment with her hand clutching Claude's bicep to move him away from me.

"Perhaps go back to where you were and keep watching," his angry voice rumbled. She looked at him as if deeply hurt by his quick rejection. This was not what I expected. I had planned to get to the king first, show him my visible proof of Claude's desires, and leave.

"She is just a widowed Baroness," she screeched, her teeth barred in anger. "Why are you so takenby a whore?" the princess cursed under her breath, and I scoffed, unable to stop myself. Even in this moment of craziness, I found annoyance. "How dare you disrespect me," the princess yelled, drawing more eyes before she reached out, slapping me across the face. Chipping away my last shred of dignity. Before I could think better of it, I grabbed Claude's stunned face, kissing him in front of the whole party. He didn't move or push me back, not even as people began to murmur. I can't believe I let the princess provoke me to this point.

I let go of him roughly, looking across the room at the king who was observing me, and I nodded once curtly before I saw the crown prince glaring at me from behind his father. "Why would you do that?" Claude questioned as he looked over my face softer than I expected but I moved away from him, ignoring him since I felt as if everyone was playing a game that I was losing, so I was done. I had confirmed with the king that Claude liked women; the prince knows I don't want him, and Claude knows I can't be trusted, so as long as no egos are indeed bruised, I should be able to keep my life.

I walked out of the party no more than five minutes after I had arrived, anxiety flooding my being, my whole body trembling in the hot summer night. At least Thomas will not have unhooked the horses since I told them to be ready to leave at any time. But just as I got to the carriage house, I felt a hand cover my mouth, my hand sliding from the door handles as I was pulled back. Janet's terrified face pressed to the glass of the carriage as she watched on, unable to help. "You shouldn't have pissed him off," the crown prince cursed into my ear before he began to drag me back into the castle through the servant's door. I kicked and fought and tried to bite him, which wasn't smart, but at this point, I knew I was going to die.

"Please," I begged, my plea muffled under his hand, but he still pulled me along, not caring as I thrashed until he threw me through a door. I had expected him to stay with me to ask me questions, but he hurled me to the floor, locking it behind him. I wanted to beg to be let out of the darkness; I wanted to plead for them to leave me alone, but I knew that was futile. I had made a gamble, but I just didn't expect the princess to get in the middle of it. If only she hadn't smacked me, I could have just proven myself to the king and left. I had really hoped that it would have deterred the prince, knowing that Claude had bedded me, but I was irrational for kissing him like that. This was what I had not wanted to happen. I need to get out of here. I need to get to Janet and Thomas to tell them to run away, and maybe I can as well. However, the longer I was isolated, the worse my spiral was into the despair of what I thought would be my death because there was no way they would let me live after this.

After what felt like a lifetime, the moon was high in the sky, and the door cracked open to let in a sliver of light, scaring me in my panicked state. “I do not understand why you had to do something so impetuous. You were supposed to be discreet,” the king slurred as he walked into the room, and I began to tremble from where I huddled in the corner, not knowing what to do or if I could run with the door now open. “Get up and take your punishment before I decide to have you burned as a witch. I am nothing but a man of my word, and I was the one who made you do this, so you will take this for bringing shame to my daughter on the day of her betrothal announcement,” the king declared, his words sloppy with drink and I stood up slowly my hands shaking in fear. “Kneel,” he commanded, and I was terrified he was going to violate me when I heard his belt come off, but then he walked around to my back. Thankfully, the first hit came. I fell forward, screaming from the pain the belt left on my exposed back, and the next hit came in the same place. “Get up!” the king commanded, and when I was able to get back to my knees, I held my chest, not letting myself fall again with the lashing. “Count,” he commanded just as the third hit came.

"Three," I whimpered, and the next came just as hard, tearing into my flesh. "Four," I sobbed before the next. This time, it wrapped around my shoulder, hitting the side of my face. "Ah, five," I trembled as I clutched my eye, and the king hit me rapidly. "Six, seven, eight, nine, ten," I wept as he struck me so hard in the head I feared I would pass out, "Please," As I reached for the light of the door, he callously stepped on my hand, eliciting a scream from me. I swiftly pressed my face into the ground, determined to shield it from another attack. "Please," I begged before the king pushed me to my side, looking down at me in contempt.

"Father, that is enough," the crown prince called into the room, and I knew if they were both here, Claude must know what was going on since the engagement was set tonight. Claude is letting this happen, so he must be just as affronted, if not more, with me. I am surprised he isn't whipping me with his fondness for vengeance.

"Remember my benevolence," the king threatened before I heard him cinch his belt back. Every loop he pulled through made me tremble more. "I will kill you next time you disappoint me. Perhaps you will have to woo me as you did to my dear son-in-law to keep your pathetic life," the king threatened, making me coil inward in disgust.

It was silent again, and I could cry freely once I heard their feet stop echoing in the hall. I lost control, curling into a ball on the ground, wishing to feel numb. I wish to feel nothing. I was so foolish for having feelings for Claude. I should have sent a letter to the king right away and not been greedy because this misery is too much to bear right now. Everything aches, and I can't move; good sex wasn't worth this pain.

The door was left open, casting light on me, but I wished to be in the dark. Everything hurt, and my pride was taken from me, along with my safety. As much as that door tempted me to run away and leave, I couldn't move. "Madam?" I heard Janet's frantic voice call out to me.

"I am here," my voice broke, and when her feet drew closer to where I lay on the ground, she drew in a shocked breath.

"Madam?" she cried as she came to help me up, but I couldn't move. "I can't believe the prince did this," Janet sobbed franticly as she tried to help me to my feet. This time, I leaned against her for support, able to get my feet under me.

"I want to go home. Just take me home," I whimpered as she tried to help me out into the hall, but with her holding all my weight, she was struggling. "It was the king...I want to go home," I whimpered.

"I will get you home. You are safe now," she comforted me as I began to slip down her arm. "I need to get Thomas," she cried, but I was too scared to be left alone as I fell back to the ground.

"Don't leave me. Please don't leave me," I begged as she leaned in to hold my face, but I couldn't focus on her brown eyes.

"I will be right back," Janet vowed to me before I watched her run away in the haze of my swollen eyes.

"Please save me," I whispered as I closed my eyes, feeling the pain take over—pain in my face, but mostly the raw parts of my back.

When I heard feet rushing towards me, I opened my eyes, hoping to see Janet, but it was Claude. "NO!" I screamed as I backed up, trying to crawl away, my whole body protesting against the movements. "PLEASE, NO!" I pleaded as I scrambled to get away from him. I don't think I can take another hit, *he is so big.*

"Caroline, stop," Claude whispered as he went to touch me, but I cowered under his enormous size.

"Janet, please save me. Please get Thomas. I am scared," I implored as she was back holding my face.

"We need to get you home, my lady. Let him help you," she appealed, but I couldn't stop shaking as my back throbbed with every move I made to get away.

"I don't want to die," I wept just as I felt arms lift me, and the pain of him touching my back made me cry out. "Please don't hurt me too," I begged as they took me to the carriage, and the whole world spun. I was in and out of consciousness, but even in the carriage, I wasn't comforted by Claude rubbing my head. He must have known. The prince would have told him.

"Why did you let her get hurt? You told me you cared for her," Janet accused him, and Claude's hand froze on my head, scaring me that he would harm her.

"I went all the way home to find her. If I had known her plan, this would never have happened," he cursed, making me flinch.

"You said you would kill me," I cried, and he flinched as his hand softly touched my bruised cheek.

"I lied," he whispered, and I didn't know if I could believe him.

"Janet, it hurts so bad I want to die," I sobbed as she knelt in the carriage to hold my face, hugging me to her.

"You will be safe at home. I promise," Claude said harshly, and I couldn't stop from shuddering at his loud voice.

"I just want to sleep," I whimpered, crying myself into a panicked sleep.

16

The Archduke's Mistress

The next morning, when I awoke, I was lying on top of Claude's chest, and from my face down to my lower back throbbed. "Why are you here?" I asked, knowing he wasn't asleep by how he was breathing. "I don't understand you. You barely know me, but spend time here like I am your mistress, and with how thoughtful you are of me at times, it contradicts with when you tell me you will kill me," I snapped as I went to move away, but he leaned up holding me to him gently.

"I know you. I have known you for a long time because of Paul," he admitted nervously, and I lay back on him at the mention of my brother. I just want an explanation for his erratic behavior and over-familiarity with me, even if this isn't a good time. His lips pressed into my forehead, and I again felt confused by his actions. "Paul was placed under me in the war and would often read your letters to us at dinner. All the men would gather to listen to you talk about the gossip of what was going on at home. Even back then, you were amusing," he stated as he kissed my temple, "Your letters were something we all waited for, especially during the winter months when the nobles here would get restless. Their antics were entertaining to us during those bleak days," he sighed before curving his body to look over my face. "I knew I had to meet you when I got back. However, I didn't know what you looked like until the first night we met," he admitted, and at least that made his behavior make more sense, even if I was uncomfortable with the information.

"The night you threatened to kill me, *the first time,*" I groaned as I touched the side of my throbbing face, wanting to turn away from his gaze.

"Yes, that night. But I went back to war, and you were married. So for ten years, I kept an eye on you, knowing that I could never be so brazen as the prince to court a married woman, and you seemed to care for Ronald. But I had planned on talking to you very soon since you only just started attending events again. I didn't know how you would feel if I pursued you, so it was truly shocking to have you come on to me so strongly," he stated as he kissed my non-aching cheek, and something in his soft tone made me believe him. He rubbed my hip as a weird tension filled the room, like a tightness between the air we shared. "I can't kill the king for what he did to you unless I declare war. I will if you ask it of me, but I am terrified to leave you alone now that people know we are an item. You are now a target, so I promise I will make him pay, both of them," Claude vowed, and I nuzzled into his chest, feeling comforted by his anger. Even if he couldn't do anything, I was just happy he would try. "If you hadn't been so hurt that I needed to get you home, I might have killed the prince right then. This was what I feared would happen if I ever showed the world a woman for whom I cared," he declared fiercely, and I was happy that he didn't kill the king or prince over what I had done.

"I deserved what I got. I am lucky to be alive, so do not worry," I whispered, my emotions slowly returning.

"If they had killed you, I would have burned the castle to the ground. You did not deserve that," he snapped, and the loud rumbling of his voice vibrated into my chest.

"I imagine so," I chuckled, trying not to feel so broken by what had happened. "So what of the princess?" I asked, and he groaned before pushing my hair back to look at me.

"I was thinking of accepting the betrothal announcement he made at the ball. The king told everyone we were engaged, so I intend to make the king suffer no heir from me. It is what the princess and king want most," Claude declared, and I smiled at the idea.

"It would be very mean to do," I whispered before leaning up to try and get something to drink from the glass beside my bed.

My lip was swollen, which made it hard to keep the water from running down my chest, but he watched me with eyes so miserable it made me feel naked. He looked at me as if someone had killed his prized horse, and it was so very confusing. "I might kill the prince for not stopping it. For a man who claims to care for you, he shows it horrifically," Claude snapped, and I chuckled at his very true words while moving slowly to get up out of bed.

"I don't know what time it is, but I am hungry," I whispered as I put on a robe.

Claude followed me down the stairs. "Janet said she had the cook make your favorite soup: tomato with cream," Claude said as he went to sit. I waited for him, uneasy on my feet. "What are you doing? Just sit," he ordered in confusion.

"It is customary..." I began, but he rolled his eyes as I slowly sat.

"I know the customs, but frankly, my dear, I don't give a damn," he grumbled before leaning over to pull my chair closer to him, causing me to stiffen in shock.

"You are so strange," I breathed just as my cook Garth came in to set down the food. "Where is Janet?" I asked, and he looked over my face with pity before passing a glare at Claude like this was somehow his fault. Thankfully, Claude didn't see because Garth is much too sweet to reprimand.

"The apothecary, the archduke, sent her with a list this morning," Garth said before leaving. I turned to look at Claude, who seemed lost in thought as he stared at his food, and to see such a large man look so troubled was odd. I didn't like it, and I have to admit to myself now that I do care for him more than I should. So I got up, wincing in pain, but I didn't like to see him so upset.

"What do you need? I can get it?" he asked as he went to scoot back, and I sat on his lap, leaning into his warmth.

"I just wanted to feel you. You are so very strong," I whispered, and he leaned in to kiss my forehead. Maybe, just maybe, he is telling the truth about liking me as well.

"You must still be high on the pain medicine," he murmured before leaning to give me a spoonful of soup, which I happily allowed him to feed me. "I should at least beat the prince," he grumbled as he cleaned some soup off my chin because it was hard to swallow with my busted lip.

"Don't be silly," I chastised him as I waited for the next bite, desiring to change the topic. "You said that you had a present for me the other day. What was it?" I asked as he fed me again, and I did my best to control my lip from letting soup spill out my mouth.

"Ahh...that...well, I have decided to just kill count La'Blauvelt at the jousting competition in a few months. That way, you can watch," he said before giving me another bite.

"So then just Halad Lasum?" I asked, and he nodded yes before giving me another spoonful of his food. Maybe he regards me as I do him? I am not too dense to understand my feelings for him are serious. "My lord, you really should be eating," I whispered before leaning down to kiss his nose, and he shook his head.

"I am in no state to eat," he grumbled before giving me another bite.

"Why?" I pressed, wanting to hear him admit to his feelings.

"Seeing you hurt makes me sick. I could have protected you. Caroline, don't do something so reckless again," he reprimanded me before giving me another bite.

"Why does seeing me hurt make you sick?" I pushed for an answer, and he set down the spoon before gently turning my face fully toward him.

"I care for you. Do not act as if this is news to you. I have never hidden my affections," he stated as if offended, and I leaned in to kiss his cheek as my body hummed from his answer. "In fact, I have been bold and shown you every chance I got how much I desire you, Caroline," he mused as he kissed my lips softly to not hurt me while his hand caressed my sides. "You are mi—" Just then, the door to the dining opened, and I had expected it to be Janet, but the crown prince had come in without knocking or even being received. The prince stood in the doorway, his shocked gaze fixed on us, and I sensed Claude's entire body tensing. I didn't know what to do in this situation, so I moved to stand to bow, but Claude held me still.

"Did you like making me look like a fool?" the crown prince shouted at us, but I felt it was more pointed at me. I figured Claude would yell or get mad, but he drew another spoonful of soup up to give to me, and I watched Claude in bewilderment as I ate the bite.

"You are ruining a nice moment. Leave before I make you," Claude threatened, and I went to stand again, but his hand stopped me, holding me closer.

"How long have you been deceiving us?" the prince roared, and again I didn't know who he was talking to.

"Tell the king to expect my official acceptance letter to take the princess's hand by tonight," Claude threatened darkly as he leaned in to kiss my unsullied cheek, and a heat swelled in my body from the fierceness in his words.

"You dare accept my sister while you court..." the crown prince yelled, and Claude stood, gently moving me to sit in the seat he was in. His mere height silenced the crown prince.

"I have fought alongside your men and been a relentless guardian of this country. My family lineage traces back to the ancient emperors, while yours is of more recent royalty. I have more men, land, and power than your father's comprehension. It would be unwise to provoke me," Claude warned the prince as he ran his fingers over the uninjured side of my face, "especially when my only loyalty to this country now sits battered by the king," Claude declared darkly, and I had to admit he probably was 6'5. The crown prince faltered a step back as his eyes landed on where Claude caressed my cheek. "You already hurt the most important person to me, for there is nothing of greater value to me. Don't make me kill you for it," Claude grinned, and my heart beat faster at his declaration. The crown prince stormed out of the room, the second time in two days he had left here upset.

"So...I am most valuable to you?" I asked, trying to break the tension.

"Yes," he breathed roughly before he kissed my cheek to brush the side of my lip. "And I should just kill them all, but selfishly, I do not want to go back to war," he admitted before going to sit in my chair, and he pushed the other soup towards me to eat.

"I wouldn't want you to leave me to go off to war. It's presumptuous, but I would like to keep you close," I whispered as I sipped the soup, not being as elegant as I would like.

"Just the idea of not sleeping in bed with you bothers me," he admitted, and I smiled at his words. *Yes, sweet and strange...*

17

Assassination

I didn't heal as quickly as I had hoped, even with Janet getting the extremely expensive remedies Claude instructed, but I was optimistic when my back ceased aching enough for me to sleep on my side. It has been a month since the prince stormed in here, and Every day after work, Claude has been in a poor mood since the wedding, and it must be quite challenging for him... I glanced at his left hand, pleased he did not wear the ring given to him by the princess. If he did, we presumably would not have the relationship we do now. "I need a competent secretary," he grumbled as he shifted papers around the dining table, and it bothered me how much work he had to do even while here with me. I know he is trying to bury the king and prince in their budget errors, and I enjoy being petty as much as the next person, but I miss him being attentive at dinner. Leaning over, I grabbed a small stack of documents to look through, and it was a basic budget report for the import of tea to the palace. It wasn't a hard task, just a lot of making sure people didn't mess up in their reports before being approved for finalizing, but Claude was hoping for errors. I looked it over, only finding a period out of place that could have changed the budget's total if someone wasn't paying attention. I marked it and placed it across his finished ones to send to the auditor before reaching for another. "Is that you volunteering?" he asked as he looked me over with a grin, and I shook my head no.

"I will help where I can, just so you aren't doing work at dinner," I said, and he let out a deep breath before pushing back in the seat.

"Have I displeased you?" he asked. I found no errors in the community planning report, so I set down the report in the other pile and beamed at him before sipping my tea. He is always so worried about making me unhappy that it is strange, yet something I deeply enjoy.

"I figured I would tell you before it becomes an issue. You are acting much too domestic, and then to bring work home seems unfair to me, *tsk*," I chided.

"*Home*?" he lilted, and I bit my lip from the misstep.

"I merely meant in my home," I lied, but he stood up to walk behind me, his nose tickling my neck before kissing it.

"I prefer it here, much less formal," he whispered before kissing across my shoulder, "the battlefield camp was even preferred compared to my palace, and here is where you are," he mused as he pushed my dress off my shoulders so he could kiss around my chest.

"Claude, what are you thinking?" I asked as my desire to have him took over.

"I am thinking when I move you into my estate, we will not have as much fun unless we keep a whole wing just for us," he drawled, and I rolled my eyes before standing up to get ready for bed.

"You are very optimistic for a married man," I teased, and he grinned at me before following me out of the dining room.

"Oh please, I know you do not care about that farce," he laughed as he came to grab my ass, and I grinned from his advance.

"Shouldn't you be at home with your archduchess? You really should mind your wife better," I poked, and he grumbled before pulling me back to him by my hip to grind against my ass.

"I would rather be deep inside my mistress," he hummed as he slowly unbuttoned the top of my dress to slide his hand down my chest.

The day he was married, I was much too high on painkillers to feel much of it, but after I came down and thought about what happened, it changed nothing between us. He wanted his revenge just as much as I did, so giving the princess a horrible marital life was mutually gratifying. I wasn't even lucid the day after, but I remember him coming into my bed to hold me on his wedding night, and even if I knew what they had to do, I was thankful he didn't smell like her. "You should really be visiting her, archduke. I can't be the only woman you bed," I teased, and he gripped my chest harder before he groaned again, pressing his erection into my ass.

"You are the only woman I want. I told you I wanted to be exclusive with you weeks ago," he whispered against my neck as he sucked and licked down my healing flesh. "Move in with me so I can keep you safe. I am terrified every time I leave you," he appealed, and I was beginning to crumble to his wants.

"We have only been familiar for two months," I moaned as his hand massaged my breast, pushing me against the banister.

"So weeks past common courting. I feel I know you better than men have known their wives of many years," he murmured as he kissed me, and every inch of me was hot and wanting.

"Claude, I..." I groaned as his hand slipped lower to pull up my dress at the front.

"You want to move in," he said as his fingers slipped inside me, making me sigh from his skilled touch. "You want me to keep you safe," I was caving as his hot breath tickled my ear. "Give in to me, Caroline," he whispered as he lifted my dress at the back, pushing his erection against my ass, "I only want you, forever," his fingers slipped out, allowing him room to fill me with his large length. "Be mine, Caroline."

"Not in the hallway," I sighed, and he chuckled as he moved in me slowly, his hands wrapping around me, holding me close to him. I leaned forward over the rail, allowing him to have every inch of me as I prayed Janet didn't come out here.

"Then say you will be mine," he whispered across my shoulder as he bit up to my neck. "In my bed," he pushed harder. "In my house," he groaned as he tilted my head back, grasping my chin to kiss my lips. "You already live in my soul," he groaned. I was losing to this man in ways I wanted; it was hard to admit, but I enjoyed the domestic side of us. I wanted to be his, and only now do I feel envious that I can never be his wife. "You control my sanity, and I am slowly losing it because you refuse me and enjoy your punishments," he crooned as he took hold of my neck, and I knew very soon he was going to turn into the beast.

"Treat me as your wife, and I will act as such. I will be yours," I conceded, and he tilted my chin back to look over my face smugly.

"Easy," he whispered before kissing me lovingly. His whole body covered and caressed me, and I felt safe as he began ravaging me. "You drive me crazy." he moaned as he moved his fingers down to my clit, rubbing slow, deliberate circles. I love when I am stuck under him, unable to move as he controls me completely. So I reached behind my head with one hand, grabbing his hair to hold his mouth on my neck, as I ground my hips back into him.

"Claude, I am going to cum," I whimpered as my legs began to shake.

"I want to hear you say you are mine," he cursed as he slowed his fingers to torture me.

"Claude, I am yours," melting into him until we both found our release when I began to shake wildly from his deft fingers. We were breathing heavily as his lips rested against my neck, and I wasn't ready for his body to leave mine, but he had to pull back to adjust himself.

"Let's get you to bed," he hummed, lifting me to carry me to the room.

"Bring the papers to bed, and I will help you finish before sleep," I offered, and he smiled down at me.

"I am in no place to turn you down. I really do need a secretary," he voiced as exhaustion returned to his beautiful face, and he set me down in the bedroom.

"Perhaps as your mistress, I can help find you someone," I said, and he nodded in agreement before walking back to get the papers while I changed for bed. Of all things, I can be helpful in that at least I know many skilled writers in my field, and he really just needs an editor to proof the report.

When he walked back in, he was grinning at me with two stacks of papers, setting the finished ones on my desk before placing the others on the bed. "I really appreciate this," he said, changing his clothes to lie next to me. "Here," and I looked to see he was handing me my glasses.

"Is there anything I need to know about any of them?" I asked, and he shrugged.

"If you see anything about Halad, just let me read it over," he noted, and I nodded before grabbing half the stack. It was nice how easy he was to be around, and in a strange way, he reminded me of my brother, only in the sense that

Paul always let me help. The fact that I was a woman never bothered him. We were young, but I hoped that Paul would have grown into a man who really loved his wife. Not many men would ever allow something like this and not second guess my skill, so it made the work go quickly.

After an hour, I was tired, and thankfully, Claude was just finishing as I leaned back, falling almost right to sleep when he pulled me into his arms. This is how we had slept nearly every night this month except the days he went home to manage his estate and bring back more clothes. He was slowly taking over my tiny bedroom with his oversized garments, but I enjoyed it and not sleeping alone anymore.

Some time during the night, I heard the balcony door creak, only to feel Claude quickly shifting off the bed. "Ah," a male voice shrieked, and when I turned to light the candle by the bed, I watched Claude run a man through the chest with his dagger. Instinctively, I pulled my rope for Janet.

"How dare you come here!" Claude roared as he threw the man to the ground, punching him repeatedly in the face. "Who sent you?" Claude shouted, making Janet rush into the room a minute later.

"Madam, are you?" Janet questioned but stopped as she watched Claude beat the man.

"Who sent you!?" Claude yelled again as he twisted the knife into the man's chest, and I was too shocked to speak. Someone tried to kill him here...he isn't safe with me here. We must move him back to his estate, where the guards are, as soon as possible.

"La'Blauvelt," the man gurgled as he looked at me in hatred, and I pulled the blanket up in fear of the implication. Count La'Blauvelt wanted to kill me, not Claude...I was to die.

"Give a message to the count," Claude seethed as he pulled the man's tongue out, cutting it off before dragging him from my room, and I was shocked by the savagery. I could hear the screaming all the way until the man was thrown from the house, and I sat in shock as Janet came to hug me.

"I think we should move tomorrow," I whispered, and Janet nodded in agreement just as the smell of blood hit my nose, making me curl forward, puking all down Janet's nightdress. "Oh, god, I am so sorry. I think the blood is too much," I gagged, trying not to puke again from the smell.

"It is okay. Let me get Garth to help clean up," she whispered as she got up to leave, and I moved to clean up after pulling on a robe. I paced the room while brushing my teeth as I stared at the blood and vomit in irritation. I usually am not so squeamish, poor Janet.

Claude walked back in a moment later, his chest heaving in anger as he looked me over to see if I was okay. "If I had not been here," he said, looking utterly enraged.

"I know. I will move tomorrow. I won't argue about it anymore," I whispered as I set down my toothbrush, wanting to feel the safety of his arms again. "What room will be mine," I asked as I held his rigid body, hoping to calm him.

"Mine. You will be with me," he declared, and I smiled against his chest before running my fingers through his sweat-drenched hair the slight smell of blood on him was nauseating.

"I see. So then, will I have to start sleeping with clothes on so your valet doesn't see me?" I asked, making him huff as his hands rubbed gently up and down my back.

"I hope not, but my staff will always be around. Which is bothersome," he grumbled just as Janet and Garth walked in.

"Sorry to interrupt, but I would like to clean up the room as quickly as possible," Janet announced, and I was happy she had changed clothes.

"I truly am sorry about your dress. I will buy you another," I offered as I turned to Janet to apologize.

"Don't be silly. It was just a little vomit. Garth set tea in the sunroom. Please wait until we are done," Janet instructed, and Garth paled as he stared at the small pool of red blood. He seemed to have the same reaction as me, and just looking at it made me queasy again. When I turned back, Claude was observing me with a surprisingly big grin that didn't make sense for the mood in the room.

"Yes, tea, let's go try to calm down," I said in confusion as I watched how he looked longingly down my body. There is no way he is turned on, is he? No, not after that..."Be careful," I whispered to Janet before I walked down the stairs, and Claude walked behind me with cheerful steps. "Why are you so happy all of a sudden?" I asked as he opened the door for me.

"I just feel as if I am getting everything I wished for...vengeance, happiness, you," he said with a smile as he came to caress my hip softly. "A man can be happy about those things even at a time like this," he whispered before kissing my forehead, and all I could do was stare up at this crazy man.

18

A Mistress's Power

That next week went by in a blur as we transferred everything out of the townhouse to his large estate, and I put the building up for sale. I had thought of maintaining it, but the upkeep would be impractical, and I would rather have the money saved for a rainy day. If one day Claude no longer wants a mistress, I won't be down and out. I would just be right back to where I was before him with how much money I'd be able to save while being in his care. "Madam, the archduke has asked for you to go over these things today," the older butler Fredrick said as he came to interrupt my solitude in the sunroom.

"Why did he not bring them to me himself?" I asked as I glanced over the list.

"Protocol, madam, and he had an early lunch meeting," Fredrick stated dryly. Even when I was a baron's wife, I hated how stuffy the staff was, having never come from a wealthy noble home.

"I see. Well, when the archduke arrives home, bring him a tumbler of whisky and tell him I miss him," I requested. I don't know if the butler detested me or not, but when he left, I swore I saw his mouth curve up into a smile.

The palace needs more 'you' in it, so when you call a designer, choose who you like, not who Fredrick tells you to.

- Get a designer to change our room and any other room you wish. I would like the sunroom to look more like yours at the townhouse.
- Can you get Garth to work with the head chef? I noticed you haven't eaten as much at dinner since the move.
- That body powder you wear. Where can I buy it? Or can you make an order, it seemed to have gone missing in the move.
- The king is throwing a party, so get a dress for Friday.
- Also, since the secretary you chose was so good, I now have Fridays off. We should pick up a hobby.
- Will you be willing to come with Lloyd and me to the races from now on as well?
- The library needs more books.

I looked over Claude's letter smiling, yes, a strange, strange man. But I could feel that he missed me as he had written this, which satisfied me. I got up from the chaise to look around the sunroom, and I could start here. It is the room I spend all my time in; the furniture is remarkably lovely already, but it needs plants. Why have a sun room with nary a fern?

I walked back down a long corridor to our room to find Janet still unpacking boxes. "Let's go out shopping," I offered, and she sighed deeply as if defeated, clutching crumbled papers in irritation.

"Yes, anything to get me out of this pile of papers we probably didn't need to pack," she grumbled before slipping on a lace shawl, and we set off on the long walk to the front foyer. Janet had assimilated well; however, we had the same grievance, the halls were too long, the food too bland with too many eyes watching us.

"Madam. Are you going out?" Fredrick asked, and I smiled at him, not knowing how he gets around so quickly in his old age.

"Yes, I need to start on the archduke's orders. Speaking of, have my chef Garth work with the head chef. It seems his highness misses Garth's cooking," I teased, and he looked slightly offended before nodding in agreement.

"Anything else, madam?" Fredrick asked, and I grabbed my parasol from Janet before looking around.

"Yes, please send out for catalogs so I can begin to decorate. Some plant nursery ones as well," I said before Janet opened the door for me to head out first.

"Have a nice trip, madam," Fredrick said as we walked down the stairs and along the formal drive lined with old oak trees that made the world seem much smaller than it was. Janet laced her arm in mine as we walked past the gardener, Martin, and his son.

"Your name is Clyde?" I called, and the boy, who was about seven, turned to look at me with a toothy grin.

"Yes, madam," he bowed, and his father stopped to watch us warily.

"I really love hydrangeas and white jasmine. Could you plant them around the sunroom and the first-floor windows?" I asked, and the boy nodded yes before his father approached us.

"The archduchess had asked for a rose garden on the west wing beside the solarium. So we will have to ask the master which to do first," the gardener said, and I smiled at him sweetly.

"There is no need. Roses take much longer, and the archduchess has priority," I stated while Janet looked about to protest, but I knew what I was doing.

"Of, course, madam. We will ask the master," Martin said as he bowed, and I smiled before leaving.

Janet scoffed in irritation when we got further away, and she appeared ruffled by the interaction. "If the gardener asks Claude, I will get my flowers first. But, if I make a stink, I will look jealous of his wife when I am not. So, the best action for me to take is to let Claude inform his staff of my authority because, as of now, I only hold the power he gives until they see me as someone other than a whore," I explained, and Janet's frown only grew. "I do not want to make enemies or life harder for Claude. I'd actually love to ease some of the weight he carries," I said, and that made Janet smile.

"You must know you love him," Janet sang as if I was hiding my feelings or oblivious to them.

"People can be silly when it comes to love…pretending it's there when it is not or not being honest about it. I do care for him a lot, enough that I would call it love, but I am not too sure it needs to be said yet," I stated just as we got to the street, and I heard feet running up behind us. Thomas was out of breath, holding his side as he groaned in irritation.

"You aren't supposed to go anywhere unguarded," he huffed as he gave me a look of irritation.

"I forgot," I lied as I strolled toward the bookstore first since that was the furthest out. Janet bristled again as people walked by me, murmuring and muttering that I was a whore that had ruined the princess's life.

"All of this because the king was curious," Janet grumbled, and even Thomas looked disturbed, but again, it didn't bother me much. If anything, people have been writing to me more often. So, thankfully, I do have some way to defend myself.

"Let's buy as many books as to fill a carriage," I voiced excitedly just as the shop came into view, and I was delighted to see the entrance because I was more fatigued from the move than usual.

"Such restraint," Janet mocked me as we walked into the shop, and I hoped that Claude meant what he said or I'd have to give him a very nice gift after everything I planned to buy.

However, I may have bought too many books, but it was surprisingly quick to do, and I possibly looked extravagant, but if I were the archduchess, this would be nothing. After having the books billed and having set up a time to be delivered at the Duchy, I took us to a lingerie shop, making Thomas stay outside when I bought a new corset and the powder Claude mentioned. I would have used it more often if I had known he liked it so much. Then we went to the dress boutique next door, and I was shocked to see Flora there and not on her side of the palace where she had hidden since the wedding. "Do you want to go do other shopping first?" Janet whispered, but I kept my head held high as the four other ladies with Princess Flora glared hot white daggers into my whole being.

"No. I only need to get a dress, so it will not be a bother," I whispered as I walked over to a lacy, off-white ball gown on a mannequin to look it over. I had seen it in the window and wanted it immediately. "I actually really like this one," I announced, and Janet didn't look to be listening as she was probably eavesdropping on the other ladies who were talking about only wearing custom dresses. But I also did not have time for that since Claude told me of the event so late.

"Madam, you should get something that is not off the rack," Janet whispered, but I shook my head just as the owner came over.

"Madam La' Blauvelt, so nice to see you," Madam Cresta said, and I really liked this woman. She was by far the wittiest seamstress in the capital.

"Likewise. Always a pleasure," I said as I touched the dress again to see its size. Could you alter this for Friday's event?" I asked, and she nodded with a grin before tilting her head toward the window. I saw Claude talking to Thomas outside—just the sight of him made my body hum.

"Yes, I'll have it sent to your new estate," Cresta spoke loudly so the other ladies could hear, and I had to stifle a grin just as Claude walked in.

The bell chimed, pulling the lady's attention, and I turned to look at him in appreciation. He was so handsome in his black military work uniform, with his hair pushed back, and when he smiled like that at me, I genuinely became weak in the knees. "Darling, what are you doing? Didn't you have a meeting?" I asked as he walked right up to me, kissing my cheek.

"It wrapped up quickly. I was on my way back to work now and saw Thomas waiting, so I wanted to say hi," he said sweetly as Janet walked off to give us space.

"Only say hi?" I flirted as I batted my eyes at him, making him grin at me.

"Perhaps kiss you, and before I forget, I got you these," he said as he reached into his pocket for a small bag. "It is candy. I had some the other day, and I figured you would like the ginger. It might help you feel better," he said adoringly as he stepped closer to me closer than he should in public.

"Thank you. I love ginger," I said, leaning up to kiss his cheek, but I stopped to whisper before leaning down. "I also got you something. Can you smell it?" I breathed into his ear, and I felt his arm hold my lower back so I could be tighter against him.

"I can not wait to lick every inch of you later," he groaned before kissing my neck, and I knew he must let me go, but I hated it.

When he reluctantly released me, his grin had turned into a yearning stare that I adored. "Then I better get you back to work," I teased, and his smirk only grew.

"If I must. I will be home an hour before dinner. Oh, can you have Fredrick take that hollandaise lamb recipe out of dinner rotation?" he asked, and I smiled with a nod.

"I assigned my chef this morning, but I will review the menu when I get home. Also, I'll remove that liver pate you don't seem to care for," I said, and he nodded in agreement before leaning down to kiss my forehead one last time.

"See you at home, my darling," he called as he left, and I gave a wave just as Janet bounced over, looking elated.

"Calm your face. That is a normal exchange for us," I murmured so the other ladies wouldn't see how smug Janet looked. It really wasn't a competition, not with Claude, and as good as it felt to have him validate me in public, I don't enjoy people watching us like a spectacle.

"But it looks to have rattled the ladies. He didn't even notice his wife," Janet whispered as I went to grab a matching tie for Claude.

"Why would he," I whispered before I opened the bag to eat one of the candies since I was beginning to feel uncomfortable with the heat of the day. "Let's get home. I want to get working on the catalogs and get things ordered before tomorrow morning," I declared as I took the tie to the counter where Cresta was also watching. "Have this sent over with the dress, please," I said, and she grinned at me as well, as if she and Janet lived for that moment.

"Also, make sure the archduchess's items are sent to the west wing, not the main annex," Janet dug in harder, and I rolled my eyes.

"It was good to see you," I said before leaving, ignoring Cresta's joyous goodbye.

When we got outside in the heat, I glanced at Thomas, who was also smiling. They must have really enjoyed the moment. "I think it's time we head home. I am feeling tired," I said as I handed him my things.

I began walking down the busy street just as Janet came out. "Madam, come on, you have to admit that was satisfying," Janet sang, and I would give her that.

"Yes, it was nice, but only because I enjoyed our moment, not because others were envious. Envy is poor company, so I am trying not to think about how I am only a mistress. Even if Claude hates Princess Flora, she is still his wife," I said more emotionally than I had meant to.

"You know why he did it. Are you not happy now?" Janet asked as she hurried beside me.

"No, I know. I just feel extremely illogical at the moment," I groaned as we approached home.

"Madam, when was the last time you bled?" Janet asked out of the blue, and I slowed, trying to think of when. It must have been not long ago, but all I could think about was a week before I got the king's letter.

"Why?" I asked as the gates to the estate came into view, and I was glad Thomas hung back, giving us space to speak openly.

"Well, you could be pregnant," Janet said calmly as we walked back under the giant oaks. "You feel sick in the mornings, are more tired, have bouts of nausea, and just now with the emotions," Janet said as if that were so easy of a thing to happen.

I tried for a child from the age of eighteen up until just over a year ago. The very night I was wed to Ronald, he said he needed an heir, so we slept together religiously, even sharing a bed, which is uncommon for married couples. It was at least two times a week and sometimes every other day. We tried for ten years and nothing. There is no way I can be pregnant. "It is probably just stress from the assassination attempt and move," I reasoned as a weird sadness washed over me that I could be reaching the age of not having children since I missed two periods.

"Madam, perhaps before you get your hopes up, we wait a while longer," Janet said as if she could sense I was going to get more emotional.

"Yes, that is smart. I am almost in my thirties. It could possibly be the end of my cycle. My mother's stopped at forty before she passed. That can not be so far off," I whispered, and that only made me feel worse. "Can you bring me lunch in my chambers and the menus to go over," I requested somberly before Thomas rushed up to open the door, and I plastered on a fake smile to walk to the bedroom, where I could cry in peace.

19

Adultery

After crying, I managed to finish up the menu before I took a nap, knowing I only had a few hours until Claude would be home. I woke up to the feeling of a hand resting on my forehead. “Are you feeling unwell?” Claude’s deep voice roused me, and when I opened my eyes, I saw that he was kneeling beside me with a worried brow.

“How do you feel about having children?” I asked, and his expression was unreadable, probably because he didn’t expect my question.

“I won’t lie to you. I always wanted them, but I do not feel lacking in any way,” he said as he looked over me cautiously.

"Janet thinks I am pregnant," I admitted as I moved to sit up, and he cocked an eyebrow up, moving toward his dresser.

"I would happen to agree, but I am not an expert," he said, and I looked at him in shock. I don't know how I expected him to react, but this wasn't even close to what I thought. "I was hopeful," he added, and I was dumbstruck by his admission.

"Um. I am sorry. But you aren't upset? And you thought I was pregnant before I did?" I questioned more to myself than him, and he nodded as he began to undress out of his work uniform. I grew distracted as I watched him pull off his white shirt, and his muscular chest came into view.

"It would pose the issue of having an illegitimate child, yet it would help Lloyd stay in control of the estate after my passing, and our child wouldn't hold the burden of the duchy. However, I am not a fan of a bastard title for our child. I could petition to marry you as well in this country, but the king would never agree. So Flora would have to *die*, or I divorce her and end their punishment, which is bothersome. Possibly we could marry in the country my family hails from...then you would be my wife in my home country," he said thoughtfully as he took off his pants, "but that would put more of a target on you both," I swallowed hard, trying to focus on his words, not his naked frame. "I guess we will have to just see how this all plays out," he declared as he put on relaxed clothes and came to lay in bed with me, rolling me into his arms.

"How can you be so agreeable about this?" I asked as I huddled my back against his chest, and his hand came to rub my stomach.

"I am versed enough to know how not to get a woman pregnant, darling, or I would have a brood running around already. I have just not worried with you, perhaps because I hoped to give you a child," he admitted. "Well, that first time did catch me off guard, but cumming in you is much better than not," he teased as he kissed down my neck to my collarbone.

"I have wished for a child for so long. I do not want to get my hopes up," I whispered, and the mood became somber as he softly rubbed over my stomach, caressing my hip up to my chest, hugging me to him as he breathed me in. Like always, I felt safe in his strong arms.

"Then let's be careful for a while," he whispered, and I didn't understand what he meant.

"I am a very lazy person. I don't do much besides sit, read, and eat," I murmured, making him chuckle.

"I meant that I would have to be gentle on your body," he laughed, and then I understood his meaning before turning in his arms to look over his face.

"You are a very unorthodox man. How does it feel like I have known you for so very long?" I asked without expecting a response.

"Because of Paul, I knew a lot about you, and the men who would write you would also read your letters aloud. Perhaps that is why it feels like that," he said, and I kissed his lips, holding myself tight to him. "Before we continue down this path, we need to eat dinner. I only came up to get you but was distracted," he admitted as he broke the kiss, and I rolled out of bed, sliding on my slippers.

We appeared relaxed as we went to eat, but I think we both were the opposite. I was emotional about a baby and turned on. I think he might be the same but in a different way. He is so strange to me. Why would he even want me to have a baby? I feel like I must have been distracted during dinner because Claude was also very quiet, and we didn't speak much, even about the day, until Janet came in.

"Madam, you have a note from the west wing," she said smugly, and I held out my hand to take the letter from Princess Flora, well, the archduchess.

"Stop looking so pleased about today. I told you I have no reason to be smug," I scolded her, but Janet only smiled more.

"What does she mean?" Claude asked Janet, and she went into the story of the dress shop for him, but the letter was more interesting to me.

-I hope you enjoyed your little show. Regardless, everyone knows that whores come and go, but wives do not.

Enjoy your short while as a novelty because, after our wedding night, I know he must think of me often.

- Archduchess Sigmund

I smiled at the letter before folding it back up to reach for my pen at the end of the table.

~Even if I am a 'Novelty,' I hope you understand that I know how that night went, so I am not worried. Please save some of your self-respect and just take your punishment well.

~ The Whore of Archduke Sigmund.

"I see. Well, I did not even notice another lady," Claude said as I handed my letter back to Janet.

"Please send this with a bottle of wine," I ordered, and Janet grinned at me before bowing out.

"What was that about?" he asked, and I sighed as I took a bite of bread.

"Your wedding night," I began, and he seemed startled as he set down his spoon to look at me. "Were you truthful in the accounts? Because she offered explicit details that don't match what you said," I lied to make sure I wasn't being played for a fool.

"I do not know what she claims, but as I told you before, I was quick and used my hand to finish on the bed. I feel guilty, but I only had to leave some evidence, or the marriage would be excluded. Regardless, I would have difficulty classifying what we did as sex. I came right back to you and held you all night. Do you not remember how quickly I was back?" he asked nervously, and I openly grimaced so he would see my distaste. "I am sorry. They also had to listen, and she drank to the point that I don't think she would remember because she didn't seem to feel much. I got no pleasure in it, and the whole idea of checking for consummation is horrendous," he groveled, and I couldn't stop a chuckle.

"Your dick was wet, and you found no pleasure?" I teased, making him frown at me.

"I honestly didn't," he declared with no hint of a lie, "I had to think of you to stay hard," he muttered as I scooted my chair back, feeling a strong need to make him only want me and I knew that feeling was jealousy. "My hand made me cum, not Flora," he continued. I know what was going on wasn't right and that some might consider it cheating what he did, but to me, revenge really was sweet. We also had not made many declarations to each other at the point of his wedding, and honestly, I didn't expect him to continue with me after what I did in front of the king.

"Caroline, what are you doing?" he asked me with worried eyes as I sank to my knees under the table.

"I want to make sure you remember me," I whispered, pulling out his soft dick to circle the tip with my tongue.

"Don't be silly. You live in my soul," he groaned as his hand came down to rub across my cheek, and he grew quickly. "I regret having to do it. If that is what you want to hear," he moaned as his fingers tugged in my mass of hair. "I don't even remember much of it. Not even her eye color or anything of significance. She was never even naked, while I remember every inch of your body," he admitted as I slowly licked up and down his shaft, making him grow. "Caroline. I only dream of you and have for years," he moaned as I sank all the way down, taking him into the back of my throat. "God, when you do this, I can't think," and it didn't take long to get him so worked up that he was thrusting into my face hard enough that my eyes watered. "Caroline," he cursed as he hunched forward, holding my head, coming into the back of my throat. "I don't know why you do this for me, but I feel like I owe you something now," he groaned as I crawled out from under the table, and he pulled me onto his lap. His face was red all the way to his ears and I felt a fluttering inside my chest from the caress of his hands as he breathed heavily against my neck.

"Owe me something?" I teased, and he nodded before hugging me tighter.

"Yes, like a horse or maybe a Piano Forte," he said, his voice still unsteady, and I chuckled at his silliness.

"I do not understand your mind," I laughed as he licked slowly down my neck to suck my collarbone. "Claude, perhaps let's go to our room. I really do wish for only you to hear me moan," I whispered, and he agreed by lifting me into his arms to carry me down the lengthy hall to the room. "I hate how long it takes," I groaned as I kissed and sucked his neck, making him more irritated with every inpatient step he took.

"I agree. We need to pick another damn room," he grumbled as he rounded the corner into the hall, the bedroom doors finally coming into view.

"Well, you walked right past the empty library. You could already be deep inside me," I teased seductively as I leaned up to kiss his mouth, and he gripped my ass tightly.

"Archduke, you have an imperial guest in the receiving room," Fredrick called from behind us, and I squeaked in embarrassment.

"I swear to fucking god," Claude cursed as he set me down outside the bedroom before leaning into my space. Pressing me against the door in his frustration to kiss my forehead. "Wait up for me. I have dreamt of you all day," he whispered before kissing my lips, his admission making my thighs tighten in desire as his hardened length throbbed on my leg—but ever so reluctantly, he had to leave.

"Hurry back," I called, and he looked over his shoulder with an aggravated sigh when I pulled my dress up to tease him with my thigh.

"I will," he stormed off to receive his guest, and even now, with him so far away, the heat of his touch was burning me.

He had been gone for a while, and I was exhausted from the emotions of the day, even if I did nap. But I couldn't keep my eyes open; reading didn't help, and no matter what I did, I ended up falling asleep. "He really is persistent," Claude grumbled as he walked into the room, and I could barely open my eyes as I turned to watch him pull off his shirt.

"Mmm, who?" I asked sleepily, and he frowned when he turned to look at me as he drug off his pants.

"I woke you. Sorry," he said before sliding into the bed with me. His naked body pulled me into his strong arms. "Tristan came to see Flora. He is upset because I do not call on her. He said they had hoped for news of an heir by now, and I think he wanted to see you," Claude scoffed, so I leaned in to kiss his strong arm that lay across my chest.

"You know it is very strange to hear their names when us lesser nobles are very rarely in the company to hear it spoken," I murmured before closing my eyes to try and go back to sleep.

"I will ignore that comment, but I had Fredrick call for a doctor to come tomorrow morning to assess you. If you have two missed cycles, I want to ensure you are okay. If it is not a baby, then I would like to know why it is happening," Claude said, and I groaned in irritation. I don't think I am ready for any kind of truth about this yet, and I don't know if mentally I am okay with having a child with Claude, for it would be much too dangerous. "Should I let you sleep?" he asked when I did not speak, and I could merely nod before falling asleep.

20

Declarations of the Heart

I know I shouldn't be so uncomfortable, but the way Claude supervised the doctor touching my stomach made it impossible to meet his eyes. This was not a new feeling; if anything, I was used to it with Ronald. He was at every doctor's visit for the first three years of our trying for a child, but I always felt his disappointment when the doctor said that I wasn't pregnant. Ronald was always enthusiastic when my period was even a day late, yet I had dreaded the next few days waiting to see if it arrived. So, the way Claude's eyes burned into my exposed stomach was unnerving. I don't know why, but I feared letting him down as well, even if this was not planned. "So?" Claude asked after a long few minutes of silence, and I gulped hard, my hands squeezing so tightly my nails dug into my palms.

"Well, it does appear she is pregnant," the doctor announced, and I must have made a noise because they both looked at me in concern before Claude put his hand out to touch my small stomach. His large hand was so gentle on me that I had to stifle a sob as I stared at the ornate leaf-molded ceiling.

The doctor is lying; there is no way that I can be pregnant—he just is scared of the archduke. "She is possibly a month or two. In another month, you will see a growth of the abdomen, and by then, nausea will subside." I couldn't stop the tears any longer as the ceiling design became hard to focus on.

"Is there anything we need to do to ensure the baby is healthy?" Claude asked. I turned to look at him, confused by how invested he was in this mess. He can not be truly happy with this; he must be lying to make me feel better. I can not believe this; none of this makes sense.

"As of now, stress can be harmful, so just relax and try not to overeat," the doctor advised, and I couldn't even imagine wanting to eat much more than what I have managed.

"And what about sex? Does that harm the baby?" I asked, thinking that was what Claude really meant with his question.

"Ah, well, we have not seen any issues with it," the doctor said awkwardly, obviously not used to a woman asking such things. Claude observed me with a grimace before scoffing.

"What are you worried that I am some insatiable animal?" he asked with a tinge of hurt in his voice.

"No. I am just very scared," I admitted, and Claude's hand began to rub softly over my stomach before he pulled the sheet to cover me.

"Will you please leave any notes for us to follow with her lady? I would like a moment alone with my mistress," Claude requested, and the doctor left quickly. "Are you okay?" he asked as he leaned me up and began to do up the front of my dress. I watched his fingers deftly button, and something about his care made me break. I sobbed into his arms, envisioning every time Ronald was let down and how inferior it made me feel. I wept for my past, I wept for Ronald, and I wept for my bastard child, for this was not expected...I cried until my face was red, and my lungs hurt from my inability to keep my emotions under control; for some reason, I was angry. I felt deep, honest anger. "Caroline," Claude whispered as he kissed my face and tilted my chin to look at him. "Do you not want a child with me?" he questioned as if not wishing for my answer.

"No, it is not that. I feel so guilty for never giving Ronald a child," I wept, and he didn't make me explain as he kissed my nose.

"I hate when you cry. It makes me feel powerless," he declared, and I let out a sad chuckle.

"You are so strange," I scoffed as I pulled back from the hug to look over his bright blue eyes. I wonder if our child will have blue eyes...

"Perhaps you are strange," he chuckled as he let go. I stood up, feeling uneasy on my feet and about my unsecured state of living. My life now is solely in Claude's hands, and it is true that once my novelty wears off, I will be cast out. Before, it was only me, but now, a child will be stuck in the middle.

"How do you want to proceed with the baby?" I asked as I slipped back on my shoes, trying to make myself presentable. "I obviously will take all responsibility since I propositioned you, and if the baby is a girl, I understand if you wouldn't recognize her as yours. I know how hard that can be on a person of your station," I continued as I pulled my hair up into a bun, helping get the heat off my neck as that uncertainty in me swelled. "But if it is a boy, I also understand if you can't acknowledge him for the sake of Lloyd and the duchy. I have prepared for the event when I am to leave, so you needn't worry about my financial care, but I do hope that even when you are done with me, your child will still remain a constant in your life. Not to say that I would seek monetary reimbursement for the child when I always wanted one, so I do not mind assuming all costs," I admitted, and when I turned back, he was staring at me with fury, deforming his face, his blue eyes dark and fierce.

"I MUST JUST SEEM AN ASSHOLE TO YOU," he snapped as he paced the room. "A MAN WITH NO LOVE OR CARE," he continued before he slammed his hand on the door when just before he had been calm. I was just trying to be pragmatic. "I have done you a great dishonor, for I had planned to give you a child from the beginning, and I *never* plan to part from you," he said harshly with guilt in his eyes before wrenching open the door to leave.

I was shocked by his admission, but not as much as I should have because of previous comments I had assumed were jokes. I watched him storm from the room, wondering if I could truly see a future with him. "You said in another country you would marry me and make me your wife. Did you mean it?" I asked, not thinking he would have heard me until he came back in with an even angrier look.

"I do not know what to do to prove to you my love and desire to make you happy. I would take you to every continent to marry you. *I want you! Dream of you! Ache for YOU!*" he yelled as he dragged his hand through his hair, messing it up.

"Love?" I questioned, and he stopped, frozen in his tracks to stare at me. "Claude, do you love me?" I asked, and his face burned a red color as he looked down at my lips.

"I didn't mean to say it like that. I had planned to tell you at a better time," he grumbled as he rubbed the back of his neck. "I will always be with you and love our children. I will protect you both with my body until my last breath," he vowed, and I nodded, feeling a tightness in me.

"Okay, well then, I will proceed as if I were your wife and you were my husband, and this is a child we had planned. But know that if you let me down, I will be okay. I will not mourn you nor suffer a loss," I promised as firmly as I could muster, only making him more upset.

"You would be okay without me?" he challenged, and I shrugged, knowing that I was lying.

"I would have to be," I whispered as he reached out to caress my cheek, and I leaned into the touch. We stared at each other for a long while as a weight settled in the room, and I realized what he *meant* when he said he had planned to give me a child. He intended to get me pregnant so I could not leave him. He was going to force me even if I had no feelings for him. I should be upset by this; I should leave him and run away to hide...but somehow, it feels strangely romantic in a cynical way, as if I might have done the same if I knew it was an option. "Claude, are you sorry for lying about trying to trap me?" I asked, and he bristled at my words.

"I did not lie. I was testing a theory, and I happened to be right. But I am sorry if you feel stuck to me," he said, shifting on his feet. I could tell he was uncomfortable.

"I see...if I am to be your *wife*, I would like a ring, please, one picked by your hand. I would also like to be married in Avadaf, where your mother hails from. Those are my only conditions," I announced, and he merely stared at me in surprise.

"I have a ring. I will present it when I get you before the ball tonight," he said the last word slowly.

"You have a ring? Like you knew this moment would happen," I chastised him, and he shifted again, his ears growing red.

"As I said, it was just a theory," he grumbled before he leaned in to kiss my nose. I moved past him, wanting him to suffer just a bit longer before admitting I was joyful.

"I will see you in a few hours. I hope I like the ring," I teased before walking off toward my dressing room.

21

The Archduke's Love

I find pre-made dresses perfectly acceptable, and of all things, I love this dress, but I know all night the other ladies will talk about how it isn't custom. Janet is already bothered by it, I can tell as she fussed over the back trying to add a ribbon, but I favored the dress. It was a simple, cloudy white with a beaded bodice, nothing too flashy. "Just focus on getting my shoes," I ordered as she tried to add a large emerald broach. "The archduke," was announced as Claude walked in in his formal black suit. I missed all his medals that he usually wore to work, but he looked so very handsome that I wished we had sex last night. "Janet, can you give us a moment," I asked as I looked over him from the mirror, and he shifted uncomfortably under my eyes. Good, I hope he has felt guilty this whole time.

"Yes, madam," Janet said as she left, and Claude rolled his eyes at her when she gave him a thumbs up. I turned fully to look at him, and he came over to stand in front of me, his thumb rubbing along my cheekbone.

"Please do not cover your face so much," he drawled, and I grinned at him mischievously. "I do not know how to do this after having it so messed up," he admitted as his hand moved to his pocket, and I held out my hand expectantly.

"Well, we can always make up a grand story if it truly bothers you," I teased as he gave me a box, and I was surprised by the age of it. It was a dark blue velvet and looked to have scuff marks on the side. He watched me expectantly, and when I went to open it, he reached out, stopping me.

"I feel I must explain something first," he began as he got down on one knee. "I never expected to use this. You once wrote a letter to Paul saying that you felt bad for me, that I would have to marry the princess. You said she is never pleased and made fun of family heirlooms, even intentionally losing them. It made me realize that I would never give this to her, so I kept it in the safety deposit box. That is why it looks so worn, but it was my grandmother's. My mother also wore it, so it means a lot to me, and I hope you will like it," he explained as he opened the boxes to reveal a massive yellow square diamond with small clear diamonds on the silver band. I was blown away by its enormity, and I felt so underqualified to even look at it.

"I don't know if I should be entrusted with something so important and beautiful," I whispered, awestruck by its size and elegance.

"It will fit no other and will be worn by only the one I love and the descendants I have," he declared firmly before taking it from its resting place and slipping it on my finger.

"It does fit perfectly," I breathed in shock, and he grinned at me.

"Janet told me your size, and I wanted to ensure it was fitted when I asked. I planned to propose at the jousting tournament after I won, killing Chal," he admitted, and I felt like my heart was going to fall to my toes.

"Claude, this is a b-bit excessive, don't you th-think?" I stammered as I touched the diamond the size of my thumbnail.

"Not really, when you consider how large the rings are nowadays. If anything, I was worried you would find it too small because it is not as large as Princess Flora's. The king gifted her an enormous ring since I didn't present her one," he said dryly. I was too shocked to care for Flora as I moved onto his knee, kissing him as lovingly as I could. My emotions on edge as I tried not to cry.

"You should have done this before Janet did my makeup," I whispered against his neck as he kissed my forehead.

"Are you accepting?" he asked, his nervousness adorable.

"You haven't asked," I chuckled as I leaned back to look at him. His blue eyes were cloudy with the same emotions.

"I guess I didn't. Caroline, would you do me the great honor of becoming my wife, bearing my children, and accepting my love?" he asked, and I bit my lip to stifle a cry.

"I will," I sobbed, and he stood up to sit on the bench, keeping me on his lap.

"I have waited longer than you know to hear that," he breathed before his tongue pushed into my mouth, swirling as he kissed me so lovingly my chest ached in excitement. "Please, forgive me for anything I have done to hurt or deceive you to get to this point," he agonized as he broke the kiss, and I nodded yes, probably not understanding the scope of his words. "I promise to make you happy," he vowed before he pulled my hand up, kissing the ring. "I love you, Caroline," he said emotionally, and I began to weep in his arms from my emotional state.

"I love you too," I admitted, and it was the first time I truly ever loved another as much as I loved myself...

22

The Prince's Revenge

I don't know how we made it off that bench or to the carriage or even the ball because all I remember is his tongue in my mouth and fingers ruining my hair. I was so worked up that I wished the carriage ride was longer or that we had taken another few minutes and shown up later. "Darling, let me fix your bun," he offered as he watched me with such desire I wanted to melt into him. "It is ruined. You might as well just take it out completely," I breathed raggedly, trying to catch my breath, and he nodded in approval before he pulled the pins to let my hair fall out.

"Here, let me just," he said, moving pieces around, and I smirked at him before launching back onto his lap to kiss him fiercely. "Darling, we should just go home," he groaned as I ran my fingers through his hair, ruining it further.

"No, no, I can control myself," I lied, kissing him harder before moving to sit across from him with a fit.

"I don't want you to," he murmured as he ran his fingers through his hair to push it back into place. It wasn't perfect, but no one would know what we were just doing.

"When we get home, I want you to do very, very inappropriate things to me," I whined just as the carriage stopped, and he frowned at me with a groan.

"I am going to die if you don't compose yourself," he cursed as the door opened, adjusting himself before stepping out.

"Compose myself? Darling, you are hard," I teased, and he pushed me so I could feel his dick on my leg.

"You really can not behave, but I like it," he crooned as he took my hand and walked up the front stairs to the door of the party hall.

Eyes burned into me, and I felt the weight of their stares land on his hand, holding mine over his arm. He was making a very loud statement right now as he showed off the ring to these people, who must know its significance by the way they had wide eyes. "I see you are still bound and determined to anger me," the crown prince scoffed as he came over to stand beside us and moved to hand me a drink. I looked at it warily before accepting it and turned away from his gaze because I hoped to see Lady Pultas now that she had had her baby.

"Perhaps his highness needs to get used to being second," Claude jabbed, and I ached to get out of the middle of this.

"So you gave her the dowager's ring. That is very risky to put a target on her like that," the crown prince stated, and I clutched Claude's arm tighter. "I don't find it to be good practice. I still am hoping she changes her mind. She would be much safer as my mistress," the prince laughed, and I wanted to stomp on his foot or slap his face.

"Well, they say it is good to have aspirations," Claude quipped as he leaned over to kiss my cheek.

"You are angering my father by being so brazen and not even escorting your wife here. She came in a carriage an hour before you *while you were...*" the prince pried, and Claude's grin only grew.

"We were tied up," I noted as I took a drink of my wine before stepping away from him to find Lady Pultas. I could hear Claude laugh as I walked off to find her sitting on a chair, holding the small baby, only a week or so old. It was asleep with a rosy cheek, so chubby I could not wait to have the same small thing in my arms. "You made such a beautiful baby," I swooned as I knelt down to look it over closer, and how small its eyelashes were made my heart melt.

"He really is just an angel," she sighed as she offered him to me. I took him as I sat beside her, holding this small thing in my arms. It was so tiny that I feared I would drop it.

"Your advice...thank you for it. I had told my father to protect me, and he did," she whispered, and I was truly shocked that Claude wasn't the one to kill Lord Pultas.

"Good. Seeing as I hold a very important secret, I hope you will hold one for me as well," I whispered as I stared at the baby lovingly. "I have been blessed to have a child. You and my maid are the only ones to know besides the father," I whispered as I touched the small pink fingers clutching the blanket.

"A child of the Sigmund line, no one would have guessed that would happen from the archduke," she breathed in shock. When I looked up, I saw Claude standing beside the king, staring at me. His eyes were piercing, and I beamed happily from holding the baby, making him smile back.

"Yes, he is a very particular man," I agree, and I was delighted to make small talk with someone who didn't hate me for a good portion of the party. But I returned the baby when I watched the crowd part for Flora to come over to us. If she caused a scene, the last thing I needed was for a baby to be in the middle. She stopped just before me with a full glass of red wine, a very bad sign, so I was glad when Lady Pultus shifted back with the baby.

"You really don't understand your place yet, do you?" Flora questioned, not hiding her hostility.

"Archduchess, my place is right beside your husband. For he is mine, and I am his," I taunted her as my emotions did a quick turn, and I lost all my tact. But she angered me when I was already nervous about losing Claude.

"You are the vilest of creatures. My father should have killed you," she spat as her drink came up, and just as she went to throw it on the dress I loved, Claude stepped in front of me, taking the entire glass of wine to the chest. The party silenced, and Flora looked devastated to have ruined Claude's clothes.

"Oh, my god! Archduke, I am so s-sorry. I did not see you!" Flora exclaimed as she leaned in to try and clean him with her handkerchief, but he turned toward me with a tightlipped frown.

"I really liked this tie," he grumbled, and I leaned up to take it off his neck.

"It will be fine. Janet can get out any stain. Remember the wine last time?" I lilted with a loving smile. "Thank you for saving the dress. It really is a favorite." I took out my handkerchief to wipe down his vest while all watched the scene in stunned awe. "I will let Janet know to launder it once we get home," I reassured him, and he grinned at me as I stilled my hand on his chest.

"I was so taken by you holding the baby that I was late to stopping her childish behavior," Claude noted, and the smile in his eyes only grew as if remembering me holding the small thing gave him great joy.

A strange man indeed, one I won't let go of.

"Archduke, I truly am sorry. I can have it all taken care of for you," Flora cried, causing more of a scene behind us.

"You have no authority in the estate, and it is Caroline's job to take care of me. You got what you wanted, to marry me against my will. Don't you think you have been enough of a nuisance," Claude said dryly, and I even felt bad for her being humiliated like this in front of everyone.

"Enough!" the king roared from his throne, and he stood with a red face. I tried not to cower or shrink behind Claude; I did not want to seem weak to him even after the beatings. "You will respect your wife!" the king commanded, and Claude openly laughed.

"You have no real power over me. When was the last time you took a count of allegiances? I not only control every soldier in the kingdom, excluding your personal guard, but I also hail from the east and the north. My family has more ties to the throne than you do. If I wanted to, I could kill you and take it like this," Claude threatened with a snap of his finger. "Control your children! *OR I WILL DO JUST THAT*," Claude threatened darkly. "I manage the finance and business section of the government. You seem to forget your place and how little power you truly have over *me* and my family, *Your Highness*," Claude's tone was terrifyingly matter-of-fact, with a touch of amusement as he reached back to hold my hand, and I watched as at least 20 men wearing Claude's house crest came to stand around us, I had no idea we were so well protected. "Expect war, for I will burn your lineage to the ground just to be rid of this forsaken union," Claude said so calmly that I believed him just as coughing began to come for Lord Halad. He keeled forward, spewing blood across the floor, and the crowd erupted into chaos as people went to help him. "Leave him!" Claude commanded, and the room quieted again, and I was even shocked by this. He never told me this was going to happen; we never got any information about him to justify the murder. "A parting gift. A traitor who tried to poison my mistress under the king's orders. Thankfully, he caused his own death," Claude said wickedly, and I smiled in delight beside him. Gosh, he was good at this game—even if it terrified me that the king wanted me dead. "I will give her your head," Claude vowed to the king.

"You dare threaten us?" the king roared as he looked at me in hatred, "I'll kill her, and if you want a war, you will..." but not a second later, the crown prince ran his father through the back with a sword. The room was silent as the grave as the king gurgled blood from his mouth in shock, not knowing who had stabbed him. Flora was wailing in fear somewhere beside us just as the prince kicked his father forward off his blade, the only sound in the room.

"I told you to leave her be!" The prince cursed at his father as he looked at me with rage—like I was the issue. "Calm him, for none of us wish to war with house Sigmund," the prince commanded me fervently, and I turned to look up at the delight on Claude's face.

"I am feeling rather tired. Perhaps we can plan an uprising at a later date?" I said coyly before he turned to grin down at me.

"Yes, darling, let's get you home," he mused as we left the ballroom into the cool night.

My body began to vibrate in shock, and I couldn't believe the king had done this after everything. "What just happened?" I questioned as he opened the carriage door for me to help me in.

"A long-awaited moment of Tristan being a man. Apparently, he does care for you more than I thought. It is surprising that he didn't kill the king when he beat you," Claude said thoughtfully as he kissed my trembling hand. "I expect my wedding to be annulled in the week, and at that point, I will take back my threat of war. As I said, I really don't want to leave you, and with Halad playing his hand earlier than I expected, this night could not have gone better," he said happily, and I just nodded along in shock. "But I am sorry I didn't tell you anything. I had no idea until it all fell into place, but you were always safe," he said as he leaned in to kiss my neck.

"So just the count is left then?" I asked, and he nodded.

"Just the count and I will make it brutal," he vowed, and I felt love grow as I crawled up his lap, knowing I was safe in his arms.

23

Little Spy

THREE MONTHS LATER

I glanced at the clock, vexed that Claude was late for dinner. He had told me he would be on time today. If he were going to be late, I would never have requested fish. "Janet, please have his food taken to the kitchen and ask them to hold mine as well," I ordered when she came in to give me a cup of tea.

"The master is home. He should be here in a moment," Janet said, and I noted Fredrick's shift in my peripherals.

"Is he really?" I asked as I turned to look at him.

"Yes, madam. The master is in a meeting right now with the king and should be done momentarily," Fredrick lied. If Travis followed Claude home, that meant he would hold him for as long as possible.

"I will go save him," I sighed as I stood up, holding my now larger stomach.

"He asked that you not be told the king is here," Fredrick declared, and I rolled my eyes. That was nearly for Claude's sanity, so he wouldn't have to listen when Travis openly flirted with me.

"Well, that seems a bit late now, don't you think?" I laughed as I left the room, and Janet followed me down the long corridor to Claude's formal office—not the one he keeps attached to our room so we can be near as we work.

"He might get upset," Janet teased, and I grinned at her.

"Well, I do hope so," I chuckled as we walked up to the door. When I went to open it, Janet put her hand out to stop me. She made a shushing sound, and we listened at the door like two silly maids.

"—already told you all the suitable candidates are being brought in for the summer festival. So I will choose a bride then," the king scoffed.

"You need to be married quickly, for I am tired of your advances at my wife," Claude announced, and I had to cover my mouth not to laugh. Travis had been unrelenting in letters after he killed his father as if that would win over my heart.

"Why must you have what I want? She should be mine, and you know it, she looks fit to be queen. If you had not gotten her pregnant before this, it would not be an issue," the king grumbled, sounding slightly drunk.

"You would be dead because she is mine," Claude stated, and Janet nodded in agreement as I blushed down to my toes.

"How unfair is the world that I never get anything I wish for," Travis groused.

"Yes, unfair indeed, king," Claude mocked him. "Speaking of, you are making me late to dinner, and I do not wish for a thrashing from my wife."

"That is not true. You once taunted me by saying that when she is upset, you get more of a high with her than on the battlefield. How can one man be allowed to have such a thing while all of us suffer," the king lamented, and Janet turned to look at me in shock. Hearing that made my stomach flip, and I was proud to be able to give Claude such strong emotions while we had sex, for I have never been to battle, but sometimes the sex is so passionate that I feel frayed when we are done.

"I told you that while I had been drinking. I hope you do not go around boasting about my wife's ability to satisfy me," Claude snapped, and I was done listening—all thoughts of food leaving me as a different type of hunger hit me.

"Go tell the kitchen we will be thirty minutes," I whispered to Janet, and she smirked at me before doing as told.

I squared my shoulder and knocked on the door once before going in to see the men lounging in the leather chairs. "I say no such things. I need no more challengers..." the king was saying, but his words trailed off when I stepped in.

"I am sorry to interrupt you, but darling, you are late for dinner. Should I eat without you?" I asked, and Claude rolled his eyes as if irritated to see me here, especially after what the king had just said.

"I will be there momentarily. Sorry to have kept you waiting, my love," he said, and I smiled at him before bowing my head to the king.

"Have a nice evening, your majesty," I said before turning to leave. "But I am no longer hungry. I will be in the library in the back section," I hummed. Claude sat up straighter as he looked me over in astonishment, but I closed the door just to torment him.

"Get out now," I heard Claude order through the door as I walked up to the second-floor library with a devious smirk. I do hope he doesn't linger after what I heard. I would really like to give Claude something to think about tomorrow at work.

I smiled at the large, wooden door, closing it softly before heading to the third floor of the library to play with him instead, so I left one of my shoes where I told I would be and another shoe at the end of a row to throw him off. As I began to take my hair out of my bun, I heard the large door swing open with a creak, and I stilled my breath, pressing my body to a stand of books to look down at him over the tops without him knowing. "Caroline?" he called as he strode up to the first set of curved, dark, carved staircases. I clutched the shelf to stop myself from laughing; I was never good at hide and seek; even as a child, my laughter always gave me away. "Caroline?" he called again before sighing deeply and going to leave. I frowned because he didn't understand what I was doing.

"Not even going to search for me, commander? Have your tracking skills been lost after no longer being on the battlefield," I teased him, slowly walking back to hide that I was now on the third floor with only one staircase down. I was trapped, so I took off my shawl to drape on a chair visible from the top step of the stairs as a distraction.

"Are you trying to provoke me, darling," he called. He must have taken off his shoes as well because, after the stairs, I no longer heard his steps. "A shoe? Are you so sure that is enough to quiet your step? You are not as nimble as you were before," he teased me, but I could tell now that he must have seen both my shoes and was heading to the third-story steps. I covered my mouth to hide my irritation at him, saying my being pregnant made me heavy-footed.

I slowly leaned down to unclip and roll off one of my stockings to set it on top of a book as I drew closer to the steps, hiding along the back wall, hoping he would first go to the seat where I left my shawl. "Caroline," he hummed, and I stilled my breath as my whole body throbbed in desire from needing him to find me quickly. I can only hold out so long before my lust consumes me. "You are much more stealthy than expected, my little spy," he chuckled from the direction of my shawl, so I took the opportunity to sneak down the stairs, but the floor creaked, and I heard him laugh, closer now. My breathing was uncontrollable as my excitement had won out. "You have no idea how hard it is going to be to be gentle on you when I catch you," he crooned, and I clutched my chest to still my breathing as I tugged down my last stocking to toss on the stairs. It was becoming impossible to not just call him to me and let him have me however he wished. But I also wanted to get to the bottom steps again to win. In my mind, I would call that a win. I snuck down to the next set of stairs to see his own jacket draped over the bottom banister, and I gulped hard. He probably has his sleeves pushed back and his hair a mess from irritation; I love it when he looks upset. Before my foot touched the top step, I heard a book thud to the ground behind me.

"Ah," I squeaked before flying down the stairs, but he didn't follow, and the second my foot touched the cool marble on the first floor, Claude appeared in front of me with a wicked grin—having dropped down from the first story. "Claude, that is dangerous!" I shrieked as I stumbled a step back on the stairs, and he caught me just how I wished he would.

24

Caught

There were no words, only us and our bodies molded together as he pushed me against the railing, taking all my air as he controlled the kiss. His breathing was rough, and his heart was beating just as fiercely as mine as I tore at his shirt to unbutton it further. "I got you, little spy," he hummed before lifting me, and I wrapped my legs around him, kissing down his neck to his collarbone as he took us to the large table strewn with books. We were tongues and teeth, hands and fire, grasping at anything the other offered.

"Do I truly give you the same high as the battlefield?" I moaned when he tugged down my garter straps with a beast-type quality that had my skin prickling before he leaned down to bite my exposed breast.

"You are much more sneaky than expected," he chuckled, avoiding the question as he moved my leg apart wider with his hips, his throbbing cock now pressed between us.

"Is it so wrong to want to know how much control I truly have over my husband," I moaned as I finally yanked off his shirt to see every taught muscle in his chest straining. He must be holding back for the sake of the baby.

"It feels as if I have control now," he chuckled as he grabbed my chin to suck down my face before biting my neck. I relaxed into his rough touch, which possessed my whole being. "But I can not deny that this feeling you give me is truly indescribable," he cursed as he seized my hands above my head with one hand before tearing off my underwear and sliding into me with the other. His head lolled back to show me his strained, flushed neck, and the sheer pleasure of him filling me made me whimper under his considerable size. "God, I ache to be deeper," he cursed as he slowly moved in me, and I wrapped my legs around him to pull him into me, not wanting any space, wishing more than anything that I was naked. I burned to feel only his skin on mine as he strained to move slowly in me.

"Please, deeper," I whimpered as my breath became hotter in the warm library, only the books to see us crash in the flickering gas lights.

"I can't," he panted raggedly as he leaned down, biting the fabric of my dress as if desperate to suck my nipple through the fabric before he stilled his hips, pressing deeper into me.

"It will be fine, please." I cried as I moved, not wanting him to stop. "I want to feel you stretch me. Your cock is so big, make me beg you to slow," I whimpered as I grasped at his open shirt to pull him harder into me, and he gave me another inch.

"Shit," he rasped, and I moved my leg up to the edge of the table to roll with him. He gazed at me fiercely as he took hold of the front of my dress with both hands, ripping it down the front effortlessly, just like when he snapped the tie. "You are pushing me and should be disciplined for hiding," he cursed as he slammed into me, and I cried out in pleasure from him finally not treating me like a breakable item.

"Claude, I got to the bottom step. I won," I moaned as I reached out to pull him down to me, lips clashing harshly as he continued to pump fiercely inside me, and I would never ask him to slow.

"I did not know that was your goal, for mine was the door," he teased a lick down my neck before biting me. I cried as I wrapped my legs around him to pull him into me. Not wanting an inch more separating us besides my pregnant bump. "So I won," he grinned against my cheek, his words burning my sweaty skin.

"We will have to agree to disagree," I rasped as it became harder to breathe, with my orgasm growing quickly, my lower body buzzing in response to his ravaging.

"God, damn, I love you," he growled as his hand tightened on my neck. "You can not ever leave me," he insisted, and I nodded with tears of pleasure in my eyes before he leaned back to rub my clit. I held my breath as my bliss began to crash around me. His other hand came to caress my stomach, and my whole body felt hot and tingled from finally getting what I wanted from him. I came hard, my entire body tensing and curling forward, but his hand that held me tightened, his body still pushing into me—moving in me quicker as he retook my hands above my head, making my whole body ache with heat.

"I could never leave a man so dependent for me," I whimpered, his teeth grazing my cheek as he seemed on the verge of his release.

"Caroline," he cursed my name, pushing into me roughly, his pelvis grinding against me as he let out a deep, guttural groan as he came. My whole body tingled and curled into him as I got pleasure from him cumming, and for a moment, I was lost in our ecstasy.

25

The Last Death

FIVE MONTHS LATER

I sat as serenely as possible, watching the men being thrown from their horses, and of all things, I didn't much like the unnecessary violence. I remember the one time Paul did it, and I was terrified he would lose his eye when he got hit in the face with a lance. "He will be fine. You gave him your needlework as a token," Janet assured me as I slowly rubbed over my larger belly, trying not to show my nerves.

"I understand, but I am allowed to worry about my husband," I spoke as calmly as I could, but I became queasy as I watched the new king knock a younger man to the ground, ensuring his victory. Tristan pulled up his face covering, looking at me with a wide grin before steering his horse my way. "He better not do what I think he is doing," I cursed before he stopped his horse at my stand, leaning up to hand me a red rose.

"The fairest maiden in the land," Tristan called so everyone could hear. I stared at him in irritation as I had to stand, which was getting harder with my body growing.

"You are too kind," I muttered as I snatched it from his hand, only making him look more pleased before riding off, and I could feel everyone's eyes on my back. After everything that happened, Claude was right. The annulment of his marriage to Flora was swift, which she still fought against. But our marriage was quick after, and with all the events, people seemed not to care about the prince killing his father; all they cared about was why the now king and Claude favored me so much. So, with Tristan giving me this flower, it will only add fuel to the fire. "He is nothing but persistent," I grumbled as I eased myself back to a sitting position just as the next set of men came out. I was so flustered by the king I didn't notice it was Claude until his name was called. I straightened up to catch a glimpse of him in his shiny, all-black armor, wielding his pole. On the opposing side stood Count La 'Blauvelt."Madam, hold my hand," Janet whispered as she grabbed my hand, which was twisting the stem of the rose over and over. "He never loses, not once," Janet tried to reassure me, and I was well aware of that, but my anxiety stemmed from my strong desire for revenge!

The horses shot forward, and as Claude lifted his pole, it left him open to a shoulder hit, but his pole went right through the head mask of Count La 'Blauvelt, and I knew his face would be unrecognizable after such a hard hit. The crowd collectively sighed as Claude circled the arena, making his way to me, and I got up to lean over the railing. When he opened his mask, I saw a small mark on his face that I wasn't comfortable with. "Are you hurt?" I asked as he grinned at me. Then he looked back at the Count, still unmoving on the ground with people fussing over him, and Claude was hailed the winner.

"Nothing a kiss can not fix," he crooned as he leaned up to hand me the rose that was tucked in his armor, and I took it, leaning in to kiss him fiercely.

"I am so proud of you," I breathed as I got more worked up from how sexy he looked in his battle armor that I forgot to rejoice in revenge.

"You should only have my rose," he murmured before looking at the now king in offense. I had to agree, but I didn't want to cause more issues by not taking it.

"Thank you for what you did for me. I love you," I said to distract him, and he turned back to look me over in longing before reaching out to rub my belly lovingly.

"I love you too, and I'd kill anyone for you...even the king," he vowed as he rode off.

I swear I should be happier about getting revenge, but I just want to get him naked.

After all, that is what started this whole thing...

The End

Mastery of Attraction

Epilogue

CLAUDE

I sat at my desk finishing the last of the day's work when the door opened, and Janet walked in with a tray. "The madam wanted you to have your tea before she came home from the park," Janet offered just before she left, and I smiled at how thoughtful Caroline was. That was something Paul talked about all the time before he died, and he might be the main reason I had been obsessed with her. Not long after he started to read her letters to us; did I realize the extent of her care for not only her brother but all of the other men stationed with us.

"She sends the best cookies," Paul said before he passed me one, and I took it happily. At the time, I had no idea what this girl looked like who sent every man in Paul's platoon a needle point for safety. Selfishly, I was upset I didn't get one because I only oversaw the men, so she didn't know to send me one, and it's not like I could ask.

"I hear she is exceptionally beautiful," a young soldier said, and Paul nodded in agreement.

"Yes, she is. We look similar, but she has black hair that curls every which way. She already has many offers for marriage. When I get back, I plan to help father pick her a husband," Paul had said, and the once delicious cookie suddenly tasted dry.

"Isn't she a bit young?" I asked, and Paul seemed to take offense to my tone.

"She has a few years, but it's better to be proactive so my father doesn't just pick the most politically beneficial suitor. It is not like we have a high status or money," he had said, and I knew that the next time I came to the city, I had to meet this girl, if only just to know this beauty they speak of so often.

However, Paul did not make it home, and the first time I laid eyes on her, I knew she was a beautiful woman, but I accused her of trying to harm me. Even pulled a sword on her, and I had never regretted anything more than that moment besides not offering her my hand before she was married. I feared she would say no and be scared of me after our first encounter, and I was mortified by my behavior. I also feared to leave her a widow, which had happened anyway. After that, I watched her whenever I was in the capital, and she had the most beautiful smile that everyone noticed. It seemed that all those around her loved to just be near her.

"Darling, are you done? Clara is down for a nap, and I thought we could go out to the garden to see the new fish in the pond," Caroline asked just as she walked into my study, pulling me from my memory.

"I am done enough," I said as I took a large sip of the tea before standing to look over her in her pale yellow sundress. She was so magnificently beautiful that I almost hated others seeing her.

"Good. I missed you today. I feel like you are always up so early," she murmured as I leaned in to kiss her cheek, and the smell of her body powder stopped me in my tracks.

"Is this for me? Are you trying to drive me crazy," I groaned as I licked down her neck, savoring the taste of the honey on her skin.

"I just wanted to remind you what you miss every morning," she breathed as I pulled her dress open at the front to kiss a line down her chest.

"You taste so good," I groaned as I sucked every inch of exposed skin, making her moan in my arms—the best sound.

Her body yielded to me so quickly until my hand slid up her dress to pull down her underwear, but she took a step away.

"I don't know if I should give in too easily. You have been absent from our bed for three days, darling," she mused as she walked away from me, and I groaned in irritation.

"I do not like to leave you," I grumbled, and she smiled as she came to stand by my desk chair.

"Sit," she commanded, and I followed her order to sit back at my desk. My body hummed from how close I was to her. She leaned into my space, and I tried to kiss her, but she pushed my chest back to pull off my tie. "Just sit," she teased as my tie slid off my neck, and she knelt to secure my hands together at the front. "If you can refrain from touching me the whole time, I will forgive you," she spoke seductively as her hooded eyes met mine, though I didn't think I could do that.

"What are you going to do?" I breathed as she stood next to me again and began to undress to just her corset. My hands already strained to touch her, and the knot wasn't tight enough to do anything but tempt me.

"Can you stop yourself from touching me, darling?" she crooned.

"I think..." I began, but my words left me when her breast pressed into my face, and I had to clench my body not to react. She rubbed against me, kissing down my neck, and I leaned into her before I could stop it.

"Ah ah ah. Aren't you a gentleman, darling?" she teased before leaning away from me.

"I won't move," I conceded, and she smiled at me mischievously before pushing to sit on my desk, her legs spread wide so I could see how wet she was. Fuck, I want to taste her, and I am so turned on.

"Claude, I was so horny all day," she moaned as she pulled her underwear to the side to slowly slip her fingers in, and I ached to do that. This will drive me mad.

"I am sorry," was all I could say as I watched her pleasure herself.

"I have to take care of myself. Is that fair?" she questioned as she pulled her wet fingers out.

"No," I groaned before she leaned in, putting her finger in my mouth, and I sucked her sweetness. Shit, shit, shit. I will lose it.

"Good boy," she praised me before pulling her finger back and shimmying out of her underwear. "I want you to feel as frustrated as I am," she hummed before bringing her thigh to the sides of my face, leaning back against the desk, her pussy so close I could smell her. I want to lick her and make her cum! I don't think I can do this.

When her fingers began to swirl and thrust into her, I couldn't help but lean in, which, thankfully, she didn't notice.

"Claude, your dick is so much bigger. I wish it was inside me," she cried as she used two fingers to fuck herself, and my face was burning along with my whole being straining to get to her. My dick was so tight against my pants that I feared they would rip before I tore this tie to pieces. "Do you want to be inside me?" she asked, and my brain wasn't functioning.

"I want it...I want to be inside you," I barely got out before she reached up to rub my cheek with her hand that wasn't pleasuring herself.

"You don't sound so sure," she teased before she reached back, gripping my hair and pulling me to an inch of her pussy, and all I wanted was a taste. "I think I should finish and let you get back to work," she moaned as she pushed her fingers in deeper, and I watched as wetness ran around her fingers.

"Caroline, I am begging you. Let me touch you," I groaned before stopping myself from moving, and she grinned wickedly at me.

"You have no patience. I lasted all day. You cant even make it five minutes," she teased before she rolled her hip up so her pussy pressed into my face. "Make me cum with your mouth, and I will let you free," she said, and I didn't need to be told twice as I began to lick and suck her clit the way I knew she desired most. She was already so worked up from herself that I knew she would be quick when her fingers clutched my hair, and she rode my face. "Claude, you are such a good boy," she praised, and my dick jumped, aching so badly to get out. I wanted her to cum on my face, so I sucked harder, moving my face side to side until her back arched off the desk and her mouth let out a silent scream.

"I want to fuck you now. Let me fuck you, Caroline," I demanded, and she nodded yes in her disheveled state.

"I forgive you. You did so well," she moaned, and I stood quickly, pulling the tie off before she leaned up to unbutton my pants. "You did well, too," she said to my dick before letting it out, and I groaned from the release of the tightness.

"Caroline, you are so sexy," I cursed before taking her neck, pounding into her as I pulled her ass off the desk into the air. I slammed up into her as she sucked and licked down my neck, and I was so close from the long build-up. "Caroline, I want to cum on your ass," I moaned loudly, and when she bit my chest, I wasn't going to make it much longer, so I pulled out, rolling her over the desk and pounding her a few times before having to pull out and cum on her perfect ass.

"God damn it, Caroline," I could barely breathe as I covered her body with mine, and she chuckled.

"You really are a good boy," she said with a grin back at me, and I never knew being controlled by a woman would be so satisfying.

Books by Author

If you like this book, you will enjoy this series.

The Goddesses in the Moon Series— Release dates

Scan me for the Amazon link

1. The Girl Who Sleeps in the Moon
March 2023

2. The Goddess in The Moon
August 2023

3. The New Moon Ascending
December 2023

Spin off

4. Tempting the Divine
March 2024

5. Taming a Goddess
August 2024

If you like this book but wish it was darker, you will appreciate this series.

The Cursed Series- Release dates

1. The Wild Prince and King of Darkness- November 2022
Angels

2. Do Not Cry For The Wicked- May 2023
Vampires

3. A Woman of Many Curses- October 2023
Sirens

4. The Wrath of the Broken- February 2024
Changelings

Scan me for the Amazon link

Search (people) Acacia Warmerdam on Inkitt.com for free books in the Beta stage.

About The Author

Acacia's journey began in a small town nestled in the gold rush mountains of California, where her love for literature blossomed. While her childhood dream was to become an English teacher, her passion for architecture flourished after purchasing a house with her husband. Now, with the freedom to revisit her love for writing, Acacia pours her heart into her work, creating engaging stories that transport readers to new worlds.

The Goddesses in the Moon Series encapsulates her diverse literary interests, blending classic writing, favorite tropes, and a rich tapestry of cultures. Adding a modern twist, Acacia injects just the right amount of spice into each successive book, ensuring an enthralling experience for her readers.

Beyond her literary pursuits, Acacia has a profound appreciation for antiques and old homes, turning her passion into a personal mission. After relocating to a remote island in Michigan with her family, she and her husband undertook the ambitious task of restoring a treasured old home, envisioning a charming and enchanting library nestled within its walls.

Fun Facts about our Author

- She not only married her high school sweetheart, but they have a true best friends-to-lovers small-town love story, having met at the age of 6.
- She has three funny and unique children who take after her unique personality, which is infectious.
- If she could, she would spend all her time with her chickens and read a book surrounded by flowers outside.
- She has always been the one people go to when anything needs to be done. Being a jack-of-all-trades doesn't even describe her well enough; she has mastered many skills ranging from baking to custom plasterwork.
- One of her most fun qualities is her ability to make others feel safe and smile even in the dark times. Her house is the place where people come to feel safe and loved.

www.ingramcontent.com/pod-product-compliance
Lightning Source LLC
LaVergne TN
LVHW051536250225
804506LV00011B/164/J
* 9 7 9 8 3 3 0 2 9 7 4 2 9 *